Also by Donald Honig

FOR ADULTS

Sidewalk Caesar (1958)
The Americans (1961)
Divide the Night (1961)
Blue and Gray (Ed.) (1961)
Walk Like a Man (1961)
Short Stories of Stephen Crane (Ed.) (1962)
No Song to Sing (1962)
Frontiers of Fortune (1967)

FOR YOUNG READERS

Jed McLane and Storm Cloud (1968)
Jed McLane and the Stranger (1969)
Up from the Minor Leagues (1970)
In the Days of the Cowboy (1970)

JOHNNY LEE

JOHNNY LEE

by
Donald Honig

The McCall Publishing Company
New York

JOHNNY LEE

Copyright © 1971 by Donald Honig

All rights reserved.

Published simultaneously in Canada by
Doubleday Canada, Ltd., Toronto

Library of Congress Catalog Card Number: 75-135440

SBN8415-2023-2

FIRST PRINTING

PRINTED IN THE UNITED STATES OF AMERICA

THE McCALL PUBLISHING COMPANY

230 PARK AVENUE

NEW YORK, NEW YORK 10017

FOR JOAN KORMAN

JOHNNY LEE

CHAPTER 1

I was thinking, as the scout sat there talking to my parents: *This is the first time I ever saw a white man in my house.* I thought he looked a little bit uncomfortable; that maybe he knew he was sitting where no other white man ever had sat before. But I think most white people are uncomfortable when they are talking to black people, like they can't ever be sure what the blacks are thinking. Or maybe he was just worried about his car parked downstairs on 127th Street. You don't like to park your car on a street where so many kids are playing, especially if you are a white man and those kids are black.

You could hear the street noises coming through the living-room windows and through the living room and into the kitchen, where we were sitting. You could hear the kids laughing and yelling, and there were automobile horns (an automobile always had to blow its horn to get through the street), and the sound of roller skates grinding the sidewalk, and the good soul music flooding out of the transistors. It was June-warm out there and I knew

3

things were as busy as a chicken yard, even though I'd never seen a chicken yard.

The scout's name was Tommy Gallard. He was an ex-ballplayer. He'd never made it up to the big leagues, only the high minors. He was about forty-five years old now. He'd been an outfielder, same as me. He told me that he'd hurt his arm and that had stopped him from coming up to the bigs. He told me that when I went into pro ball I'd have to look out for injuries, because there was so much chance of it. Young ballplayers stood the biggest chance of hurting themselves, he said, because they didn't have experience and sometimes tried to do things in a hurry.

He had questioned me kind of close one day in the park, between games of a doubleheader. He had been coming out to our park league games pretty regular during the spring. I'd pegged him for a scout right off, though some of the other fellows said no. But I watched him close. He did things that only a scout would do. For instance, now and then after the pitcher had released the ball he would keep his eyes on the pitcher instead of following the ball like everybody else did. Only a scout would do that, be interested in a pitcher's follow-through. Then sometimes he would move around, watching the game from behind first base, then from behind third, then from right behind the batting screen. Those are things that only a scout does.

Then I knew he was watching me. He went behind the batting screen whenever I was up. I could feel him staring at me. I had some pretty hot days, was hitting the ball real good, and I knew I could run and had the arm.

4

And I was trying extra hard, hustling on everything, because I knew he was there.

Then one day he came up to me between games. I was sitting on the grass drinking a root beer. I'd had a sweet first game—two triples, a back-handed catch in center field, and a few good clothesline pegs. I'd done real sweet, and now here he was.

He asked me my name, how old I was, where I went to school, when I was graduating, when I'd be eligible to sign, did I want to play pro ball, and things like that.

Then he said, "Do you smoke, Johnny?"

I knew what he meant by that.

"No," I said.

"That's good," he said. "Do you drink?"

I held up the can of root beer.

"Here it is," I said.

He told me he was a scout for the big team here in New York and that he had been watching me play. I told him I'd been watching him watching me. He didn't smile. He never smiled. His face was always set and serious.

He asked me if any other scouts had spoken to me.

"No," I said.

"That's an honest answer," he said. "Most boys lie about it. They figure they'll get a bonus if there's a competition."

"Maybe I should have lied too, huh?" I asked.

"No," he said. "Don't ever lie." He was so serious.

When I went home I told my mother about it. It didn't seem like such a big thing to her at the moment. My older brother Howie was in Vietnam, my next older brother Norman was having wife trouble down in Delaware where he was living, while my younger brother Jesse was in the hospital with a broken leg which he had given himself in a fall from a bicycle—which he had also given himself (that boy got into trouble sometimes).

So it was my father who was most interested. He was a big baseball fan anyway. He could remember Jackie Robinson's first game and things like that. He told me that he would sign the contract if I wanted him to (I needed his permission because I was only seventeen years old).

So Tommy Gallard came around right after I graduated from high school and sat down in the kitchen where no white man had ever sat before and sipped the coffee my mother had made. He laid the contract on the table. It was folded over so only the cover showed. I could see the team's name on it, in print, and my name in typewriter print. Ma and Pa were looking at it same as me, but nobody made a move to touch it. Everybody knew I was going to sign it no matter *what* it said.

"Johnny will be paid four hundred fifty dollars a month," Tommy Gallard said.

I shot a quick look at Pa's face; that was more money than he was earning every month at the moment. He knew it, so did Ma. But they didn't show anything, not even the wink of an eye.

But the money wasn't important to me at all, even though it was going to be nice to have some rattling around in my pocket. The reason I wanted to go into the professionals was because I wanted to work my way up to the big leagues. I'd made up my mind when I was five years old that I was going to play in the big leagues.

6

It took a while for my mind to convince my body though, because when I was twelve I was so skinny my friends called me "Pencil." Then all of a sudden I started to fill out and next thing I knew I had height and weight and muscles and could really feel the strength growing in my body, the speed in my legs, and most of all I began to feel the terrific confidence you get when you know your body can do anything your mind wants it to.

Another reason I wanted to go into the professionals was because they played every day. Nobody else, nowhere else, was at it every day like the professionals. And not only that. They had more than one or two baseballs for a game, and they all wore the same uniforms, and the fields had fences and real foul lines and the bases were strapped down, and people paid money to watch the games. I knew a guy on 138th Street who had played two years of minor league ball in the Midwest and he told me a lot about it.

I played for my high school and on Sundays with a team in the park league called the Harlem Black Cats. The worst thing that could happen was for it to rain on Sunday. We played a non-league game one Saturday at a place called Victory Field in Queens and I hit a ball they said went four hundred feet. Too bad there wasn't any scout there *that* day. I asked if I could have the ball after the game for my memory shelf, but the home team said it was the only one they had and I'd have to pay them for it. That's what happens in amateur ball.

I was wearing my glove now, punching the pocket with my right fist. Tommy Gallard was answering the questions my folks were putting to him. He told them that the reason the big team was sending me out now, in

June, in the middle of the season, was because they thought I was good enough to break right in, without waiting for spring training next year. They liked to break in the especially talented ones as quickly as possible, he said. That's just how he said it too: the especially talented ones. I made out I wasn't listening, just sitting there and punching my glove, not looking up.

Then he asked me if I'd ever been away from home before.

"No," I said.

"So you haven't traveled much."

"No."

I didn't care about travel. All I was thinking about was putting on a uniform and being a professional baseball player, and living the life that went with it. I'd live in a hotel and eat in restaurants and play under lights (they played all of their games at night in the minor leagues, except for Sunday and sometimes Saturday), and get my name in the paper and give autographs and be known to people. But most of all I'd know every morning when I woke up that I was going to play a ballgame that day, and that if it rained I wasn't going to have to wait for a whole week to pass before the chance came to play again.

"We've decided to send you to our Proctor farm team," Tommy Gallard said. "It's a Class D league— the Mountain League—and probably a good place for you to break in. The team can use some help. Especially in the outfield. You'll have a chance to play, that's the main thing."

"Where is Proctor, Mr. Gallard?" my mother asked.

"Proctor is in Virginia," he said.

CHAPTER 2

I had to change buses at Washington, D.C., and wait for two hours in the terminal to connect with the bus that was going to Proctor.

The club had sent me a bus ticket; they said it was the only way of getting to Proctor. When I told some of the guys that, they laughed and said, "Man, you mean to tell that planes and trains don't go there?" We went to the Shell station and got a map of those parts of the country and looked for Proctor. We found it finally, after tracing our fingertips up and down across the face of Virginia for maybe ten minutes. It was way down there, not far from where Tennessee began, and not far from North Carolina, either.

"Well," I told them, "at least it's on the map." That was about all you could say for it, too. It just seemed to be sitting way down there in Virginia, not near anything special. It didn't have any of those little scraggly black lines going through it like most places on maps do.

"You be careful getting off at Proctor," one of the guys said. "The bus probably doesn't stop there."

They all laughed hard at that. We were sitting on the stoop downstairs, late at night. I was leaving that next morning. We'd been throwing a baseball around until ten o'clock at night, by the bright of the streetlights.

"They say there's thirty-five people in Proctor," said another one, "counting them that's in the cemetery and them that's passing through."

"Who's 'they'?" I asked.

"I'll tell you who 'they' is," said a skinny guy we called the philosopher. "When *they* is talking about 'they,' *they* is talking about you, man."

"Far as I'm concerned," I said, "*they* is the pitchers. Those are the boys I got to look out for."

We sat there and jived and laughed until one o'clock in the morning, until Old Man Herbert on the first floor put his face in the window and told us to button up or go away. He'd been nervous and cranky ever since somebody robbed his house and stole his watchdog.

I was wishing some of the guys were there with me as I walked around the bus terminal in Washington, D.C. I guess everybody gets lonesome walking around a strange place.

I wanted to take a walk around the city and maybe see the White House and the Senate and those things, but I was afraid I might miss the connecting bus, so I stayed in the terminal and looked at the people. Everybody was hurrying about, swinging their luggage.

I felt special, being a baseball player, like I was already a big leaguer. I all of a sudden felt older, too. Maybe it was because I had signed my name to a contract; was a professional. Or maybe it was because here I was, away from home by my lonesome, in the bus terminal in Washington, D.C. But whatever was the push, I had begun to feel different.

I held tight to my suitcase. My father had warned me that there were people in bus terminals who made a business out of stealing luggage. I had my spikes and glove in the suitcase and sure didn't want to lose them. You don't have spikes and glove, man, you're no ballplayer.

My mother had made me sandwiches and I ate them now, sitting on a bench, using my suitcase for a table. I kept watching the clock. I don't think my eye was ever away from a clock for more than a minute. The last thing in the world I wanted was to miss that bus.

There was a woman sitting across from me with two little kids curled up under her arms sleeping. I couldn't have slept for anything just then. I didn't think I'd be sleeping for the next five days, I was so excited.

Well, I didn't miss the bus. The minute I heard it called out on the loudspeaker—it was spoke of as the Knoxville bus, with stops at places like Charlottesville and Roanoke and others, including Proctor—I ran to the gate. I was the first one on.

I didn't see much of Washington from the bus window. They take routes that don't allow you to see much of the city. I would've kept my nose stuck to the window anyway—I wanted to see everything—except that the guy sitting next to me felt talky.

"Where you heading?" he asked.

"Proctor, Virginia," I said. "I'm joining the ballclub there."

"Ballplayer, huh?" he said. "Well, that's not my game. I like to bowl. Bowling. That's my game."

He was an old guy, with gray hair mowed down as flat as the hair of a carpet. He told me that once he bowled 215. He had the whole game memorized, just how he hit down all the strikes and clipped off his spares. I didn't care much for bowling. Nobody that I knew ever went in for it. But I listened polite and let him gas away. When I got the chance I asked him how come he didn't like baseball.

"I never could play it," he said.

"Well," I said, "it isn't easy."

He got off in some little town and the seat stayed empty for a time. Then, later, somebody else took it. This was a black woman, a grandmother type. She smiled at me when she sat down and then took to reading a book and never said a word. This gave me the chance to look out the window again.

It started to get dark when we began rolling through the Blue Ridge Mountains. I'd never seen such a spread of mountains. They reached out as far as you could see, smooth and dark. I'd been up to the Catskills a couple times but they weren't anything like this. These mountains looked like they'd pushed the rest of the world— cities and people and buildings—way far back out of sight.

Soon it was pure night outside, the kind of nightness you never see in New York City. In New York, no matter how late it is, there's always a lot of lights somewhere. But here, in the Blue Ridge Mountains, there was a blackness as pure as coal. You got the feeling, too, that there wasn't a sound out there, that those mountains rolled away into the night for a thousand miles and there wasn't one whisper of sound or wink of lights all through them.

We stopped for a rest break at some little roadside place. It was good to get out for a leg-stretch. The air was cool and just a little bit sharp. I took a couple deep breaths and realized I'd never breathed such air in my life. I'd read in the papers and heard on television about air pollution in the city but had never thought much about it. But now it came to my mind that it must be true, because this air tasted so clean. It goes to show that you don't really know how bad something is until you get to a place where it isn't.

I stood there for a few minutes just breathing the air. The night mist was burning in the beams of the bus's headlights which were shining out like two monster eyes. Everybody else had gone into the restaurant and I was about to go in too when this girl came up to me. She had been on the bus since Washington. She was a white girl, kind of tall and skinny, with blond hair that hung straight down over her shoulders. She wore glasses and had small thin lips.

"Would you like me to get you something?" she asked.

"Pardon me?" I said.

"Would you like me to get you something?" she asked again.

"I was just going in."

"They won't serve you," she said.

"I've got money. They'll serve me. I'm with the bus," I said.

"You don't understand. You've never been south before, have you?"

13

"No," I said.

I started to head for the restaurant. She walked alongside me.

"This is backwoods south," she said. "They're still behind the times here."

I stopped outside the door and looked in. There were people sitting at a counter and at tables. Through the screen door I could hear them talking and there was the sound of dishes and cash register and things like that. Country music was on the juke box. I didn't see any black people in there; but there weren't any on the bus, besides me.

"Don't go in," the girl said. "Maybe you shouldn't go in."

It was mostly bus people in there, with some locals sitting off in a corner not doing anything but staring at the others. I guess this was the big event in the neighborhood—the bus pulling in.

I was asking myself now if I really wanted something. I'd been thinking of a cup of coffee for the last half hour. But did I really want it? Then I told myself, Yes, I did. Because I found myself thinking: Look, boy, all you did was ride on a bus for some hours. You haven't crossed no borders or no oceans. You want coffee. They sell it here. So don't think about wanting, only about getting.

When I opened the door and stepped into the small by-the-road restaurant tucked away into the mountains of Virginia, I found myself expecting something to happen. I thought sure it was going to become a scene out of a movie, with the music stopping and all the people freezing in what they were doing to stare at me. I knew something about discrimination, of course. They've got it in

New York the same as anywhere else, only in New York it has manners; it's polite and smiley and has butter on it, and you find yourself laughing at it because it doesn't think you can spot it. In New York they have people who call you spade to your face because they think they're so far away from being prejudiced that they can freely say this to you. In the South it's different. First off, their hangups are called bigotry, which isn't as smooth a word as discrimination. And second, it's meaner than in New York. It doesn't smile. It burns on a very short fuse. If I had to choose between discrimination and bigotry, I'd still take freedom.

But all the same I went in there, with the girl behind me. I wished she wasn't there, wasn't so interested. She was very tense, like she was waiting for something to happen, almost as if she *wanted* something to happen, just to prove her right. I knew what would take place, too, if some honest bigot called me a spade and threw me out. She would become the Public Defender and make a fuss. That's all right too. There's a time when you got to make a fuss. But if you don't figure it real careful before it starts, then you're not going to get anything out of it.

Well, no music stopped and nobody froze up when I got to the counter. I knew the locals were looking at me, but I pretended not to know of them. There were two people working the counter, an old man and a young girl. I asked the old man for a container of coffee. (I said that without hardly knowing it. I thought I was saying cup but it came out container.) The old man looked at me for a second. His eyes kind of stopped in his head for a second and studied me out. Then his eyes got used to looking at me, kind of. It took him only a second.

"Cream and sugar?" he said.

"That's right," I said.

He gave it to me and I bought a flat little piece of cake wrapped in cellophane and went outside. I stood out on the edge of the road and drank the coffee and ate the cake. Once in a while a car came shooting past, but mostly the night stayed locked dark in the mountains.

It wasn't far to Proctor now and I was getting more and more anxious to be there. Why, tomorrow night this time I might be playing professional baseball.

CHAPTER 3

I hadn't figured on getting into Proctor at twelve o'clock at night. But the bus had lost time coming out of Charlottesville and then again at Roanoke, so here I was.

I hadn't exactly expected a brass band, but you sort of dream (after all, man, that was a long, long bus ride and you don't have much to do but sit and think) of the sportswriters being there to meet you and catch your first words. After all, Tommy Gallard had said the team needed help in the outfield, and here I was, come down all hot and ready from the big city to give them help.

I was the only one to get off the bus in Proctor. And if I hadn't signed a contract I wouldn't have got off either. There wasn't even a bus terminal. The bus just stopped somewheres along the main street, just like the buses on Lexington Avenue, and let me off. Then it went away. I stood there holding my bag watching it go away into the night. That was a lonely feeling.

There wasn't much going on in Proctor at that hour. In fact, I was the only one on the street. There wasn't a person to be seen, or a store open, or a light going except for the streetlights. It was the first time I had ever seen such an empty street and it was the wildest feeling. In Harlem you can hardly see the street for the people, and there's always noise and music and lights. But here there wasn't a sound, not the slightest peep on the air. I stood there looking both ways, up and down the street, and I could hear my neck rubbing on my jacket collar when I turned my head.

On either side of the street were stores. Some of them had apartments over them and some didn't. Looking up, I could see stars. I had hardly ever seen any before. So this was where they were. The whole sky was done up with them. And then I noticed another thing that was fresh to me: there weren't any cars parked on the street. Not a one. Well, I thought, no wonder there's nobody on the street—they don't have anyplace to lean against. This town Proctor was something else all over again.

Behind me was a store that had the name of the bus company on the window. But it was closed. Everything was closed. The only thing that was moving was the traffic light down at the intersection on the next block. It just kept going, red and green and green and red, without any cars to pay attention to it, like it was just giving itself a workout.

Tommy Gallard had given me a piece of paper with the manager's name and address on it. I was supposed to look him up the minute I hit Proctor. He was expecting me. But I didn't think he was expecting me at twelve midnight and I gave myself credit for having more sense than to wake up a man I didn't know at twelve midnight. Especially when I was going to work for him. His name was Lloyd Rosewell. He was a playing manager, a first baseman.

Then I saw headlights coming along the street. It was the first thing that I'd seen moving in Proctor. And I knew what kind of car it was too. It had the same slow, prowling look to it that they had in New York. Sort of *easing* itself along the street.

I waited for it to come up to me. This was one car that wasn't going to pass me by without stopping. No sir. I was standing there like a stop sign.

It stopped in the middle of the street, even with me. There were two of them sitting inside, in the dark, both looking at me. The one who wasn't driving was closest and he called out to me.

"What are you doing there?"

"Nothing," I said.

"Come over here," he said. He wasn't particularly unfriendly. His voice was kind of neutral. I picked up my bag and walked into the street and up to the car. It had County Police written on the side, inside a big star. The car was picking up shots of streetlight on the hood and roof, like it had been Simonized that afternoon.

"What are you doing?" the cop said.

He was wearing a cap with a visor and a blue shirt that was open at the throat, and a badge. He was skinny, with flat little eyes. His lips hung apart when he wasn't talking and you could see his kind of long teeth.

"I just got off of the bus," I said.

"Why?"

"Why? What do you mean, why?"

"I want to know for what reason you got off the bus," he said.

"Because my ticket said Proctor," I said.

"I see," he said.

Now the other cop, the one behind the wheel, leaned his head forward and looked up at me and said:

"Why'd you get off here?"

"Because this is where I was coming," I said.

"But you're just standing in the street."

"I didn't figure on getting here so late. The man I got to see is probably sleeping."

"Who do you want to see?"

"Lloyd Rosewell."

"You a ballplayer?"

"I'm Johnny Lee," I said. "I'm the new outfielder."

They both looked at me straight on for a couple of seconds.

"Rosewell's probably sleeping by now," the skinny one said. "You'd better wait to morning before going there."

"But where can I go now?" I asked.

They looked at each other. Then the skinny one said:

"You can try the hotel." He said it in such a way as not to make it sound encouraging, the way his voice laid under the word "try."

They told me how to reach the hotel, then rolled off in that slow steady way.

The hotel was the tallest building in town, six floors high. It was called the George Proctor. It stood back from the street and had a lawn and neat-looking shrubberies in front, with spotlights up from the lawn shining on it. I was beginning to get tired and was feeling lonesome, too, walking around a strange town at that hour. So I was really hoping to get a room. But the minute I walked into the lobby I got the feeling that they weren't going to want me clashing with their white sheets and pillow cases.

The lobby was empty except for a tall thin cat standing behind the desk. He was a real old-timer, maybe seventy. He had thick gray hair which he combed straight back on the sides and kind of a puffy red face that seemed to bulge up and narrow his eyes. When I got close to him I could see all the little red veins in his cheeks. He was dressed real fine, except that his suit was a cut from some long-ago yesterday. I never notice styles of wear as a rule, except when they're from thirty years ago or from tomorrow. This one was definitely not tomorrow—unless somebody was having an idea to bring it back.

He didn't say anything, just watched me walk in through the door with my bag. I came across the carpet and marched up to his desk and already I was wondering if I would be able to find a nice soft park bench someplace.

"I'd like a room for the night," I said.

"We're full up," he said, very quiet, right off the edge of his lips.

"Nothing at all?" I asked.

"Full up," he said, lifting one eyebrow over it this time.

"Is there another hotel in town?" I asked.

"No."

"No place to stay?"

"This is the only hotel."

"I'm with the baseball team," I said, trying to crack some ice. "I'm the new outfielder. Johnny Lee."

That didn't make much noise with him either. He kept staring at me. I've seen livelier faces on postage stamps.

"Can I sit in your lobby till morning?" I asked.

"We do not permit loitering."

"I'll pay."

He didn't even bother to say No again. He was the tightest uptight cat I've ever seen. He just kept his eyes fixed on me. He had real bullets in them, too.

So I left the George Proctor Hotel and went back outside. I walked along the main street again, past all the empty stores, listening to the beat of my own footsteps. My suitcase was starting to get heavy. I didn't have any idea of what to do except walk on the main street.

Then here it came again, from the other direction now. Slow and easy, like it didn't have a motor and was being pushed along. It stopped.

"No luck, huh?" the driver said.

"No luck," I said.

"Get in then," he said.

Well, I thought, here it was. My first night in town and I was being busted. That was going to look real bright on my record.

"I didn't do anything," I said.

"You just get in here," he said. There was business in his voice this time.

So I walked into the middle of the street (out of habit looking both ways for traffic, though I'll bet there wasn't another car about for fifty miles) and opened the back door of the police car and got in. Then they started rolling again.

The skinny one turned around and looked at me.

"We're taking you to jail," he said.

"Listen, I didn't do anything," I said. "What do you want to do that for?"

"You're a menace on the street, boy," the driver said.

"That's right," the skinny one said. "Safest place for you is the lockup."

"Can't I call Mr. Rosewell?" I asked.

"You cannot, no sir," the driver said.

The jail wasn't far away. Nothing in Proctor was far away. We pulled up in front of the police station, which was a small brick building. We went inside. A fat man wearing a badge on his blouse was sitting behind a desk. He was mostly bald, though I'll bet not more than thirty-five years old. He had four pens clipped onto his shirt pocket. This was the kind of southern cop they showed in the movies, fat and mean. He was smoking a cigar.

"What's this?" he said.

"This is Rosewell's new outfielder," the skinny cop said. "Just off the bus. He's got no place to sleep. We're going to bunk him for the night."

The fat guy behind the desk looked at me and said, real nasty:

"You'd better get yourself a place to bunk, boy. We ain't gonna give you room and board every night. This ain't no charity organization."

I didn't say anything. I could see he was stupid. I followed one of the cops down a little corridor where there were four cells. Each one was empty. The cop opened one of the doors and told me to go in and go to sleep.

"You ain't arresting me?" I asked.

"Who said arrest?" he said. "You got a guilty conscience or something?"

"Not me," I said. "I just want to play baseball."

He started to go away, closing the cell door.

"Hey," I said, "you're going to let me out in the morning, aren't you?"

"Sure," he said. "Unless you commit some crime in there during the night."

Then he went away. I put down my suitcase and stretched out on the bunk. It hung from the wall by chains and was hard as a board. Well, I thought, here I am, my first night in town and already I'm a guest of the county.

CHAPTER 4

When I got out of jail in the morning I went straight to Lloyd Rosewell's house. He lived around the corner from the main street, in a neat two-story house. There was ivy growing over the front porch. I walked up the porch steps and here was an old guy sitting in a rocking chair in the corner, sort of looking across his shoulder at me.

"What you lookin' fer?" he asked.

"Mr. Rosewell," I said.

"What's your name?"

"Johnny Lee. I'm an outfielder."

The old guy got up and headed inside. He had a shaggy, bumpy, old man's walk.

"You wait here," he said.

I put my suitcase down on the porch and sat on it. It was a sweet, slow, warm day. Birds were singing in the trees in front of the house. Proctor had shown some life this morning. The stores were open and there were people on the streets and cars moving up and down the main drag, which was called Jackson Street. It had been nice to finally see people other than the cops and the dummy from the hotel.

I heard somebody coming and got up. Well, it looked like I had broke him out of sleep after all. He was coming through the doorway toward me just tucking in his shirt in the back, his big arms reaching behind him. His hair wanted a comb and his face wore that disgruntled look which comes when those last five minutes of sleep have been denied. When he came out to the porch his eyes looked up into the sunshine like the air had a sour taste. Then he looked at me.

"Johnny?"

"Yes sir."

We shook hands.

"I'm Lloyd Rosewell," he said. He had a great big strong hand. He was the manager all right. He was about thirty years old, if you can ever tell what anybody's age is.

"When did you get in?" he asked.

"Late last night."

"Where'd you stay?"

"In jail. The cops let me sleep there."

He didn't seem to think anything about that.

"You have breakfast yet?"

"No sir."

"Come inside."

I followed him in and we went to the kitchen. There was an old lady there, and the old guy from the porch was there too. They just looked at me, never said anything. Here was the black plague right in their own kitchen but they kept shut about it, because it was Rose-

26

well who had brought me in. I put my suitcase down and took a seat. Rosewell asked the old lady for a couple of breakfasts and she went about making them. The old man cut out, probably back to the porch.

"Tommy Gallard wrote me about you," Rosewell said. "He said you could play ball. Can you hit?"

"I was doing pretty good," I said.

"Well, that's on the sandlots. There's a big difference between the pitching you saw there and what you're going to see here."

He was southern. Not deep south, but somewhere midway, as far as I could tell. Tommy Gallard had told me about him. He'd been in the minor leagues ten years, once getting up to Double-A ball. Now he was a playing manager. He had a tough way about him. I couldn't tell how he felt about me; you can't always tell with a fellow who has a tough way about him. But either way, he was stuck with me. The big team had sent me. But for the moment I didn't care too much about any of that. All I wanted was a feed; I was as empty as a basketball inside.

The old lady fixed us eggs and toast and coffee. I could have gone in for seconds, but I didn't say anything.

"We need hitting," he said while he drank his coffee. "We've got the pitching this year, but we're weak with the stick. Can you play center field?"

"That's where I've been."

"You've got to take charge out there you know. I like my center fielders to move. They're supposed to go after anything they can get their hands on. If you can't cut it we'll put you in left field. We need a bat in the outfield."

He went on to tell me how he wanted the club to do well this year, that it was important. I knew what he meant by that: important to him. He didn't want to go on managing in the boondocks all his life. If the club had a good year it would make him stand taller. The organization moves their managers up same as they do their players.

Then we were ready to go. I thanked the old lady for the feed and she said I was welcome, said it at the sink with her back to me. I picked up my suitcase and followed Rosewell out.

We went to the team office, which was in a room upstairs from a store on Jackson Street. There I met the team's secretary, Mr. Clidell Hapgood. He was sitting behind an old desk. He looked to be in the middle of his time, about forty-five or fifty years old, with slicked-down hair and the look of a hunter in his little eyes. He had a very small, very thin mouth, no more than a razor edge of it. I didn't like him straight out and I could tell what he thought of me. We didn't even pretend we were going to shake hands.

"We've got to find you a place to stay," Rosewell said as he shuffled through some mail. Hapgood kept his little eyes fixed on me like I was television.

"Any suggestions, Clide?" Rosewell asked him.

"That ain't my department," Hapgood said.

Then Rosewell looked at me, steady, like a man looks at you when he doesn't think you can see him. But he was looking right at me, his hand touching his chin. One thing he was thinking, I was sure: he was wishing I was white.

"We're going to have to get you a place to stay," he said.

I just nodded to him.

"Lloyd," Hapgood said. "Who you goin' to cut?"

"Spence," Rosewell said.

"Ah," Hapgood said, quiet. "You told him yet?"

"I'll tell him tonight."

I knew what that was about. He was going to have to drop somebody from the club in order to put me on. He had to do that, whether he liked it or not. The club could carry only so many players. I didn't like the idea of somebody going on my coming, but there wasn't anything I could do about it.

I left my suitcase in the office and went out with Rosewell. Everybody in town knew him. Wherever we walked they said hello to him. It made me feel good to be walking with him. They all knew him, white and black. The black people looked most curiously at me; the whites didn't bother a second look. But the black people knew right away here was a new face in town, and walking with the manager of the team, too.

He took me around to a couple of rooming houses and tried to get me in. Each place it was the same. They took one look at me and told him they were full up. Rosewell didn't argue it. He understood. I understood too. I was beginning to wonder if I was ever going to find a place to sleep in this town besides the jail.

"Where do the other players stay?" I asked.

"They're scattered around town, in rooming houses, private homes."

So we went back to Jackson Street and he told me

that he had some things to attend to. He said something would "work out" about lodgings and that I should report to the ballpark at six o'clock with my gear. Then he went about his business.

I would have gone about my business too, except that I didn't have any. I began to walk up and down the street, looking in the store windows and watching the people. It was a quiet town, even at high noon. There was a five and dime and a big grocery store and these got most of the trade. There was a movie house but that didn't open until six o'clock.

Some of the people on the street looked different from others. These were (I found out later) the mountain people. They lived up in the mountains and had little patches of land and came into town every so often to buy things. Some of them were kind of rough-looking and you could see that they didn't mix too well even with the local people. They had tough, unfriendly eyes for everybody, white and black. They drove pick-up trucks or dusty cars and a lot of them wore overalls and ankle-high work boots. They all looked kind of scruffed and beat up with work and even the younger ones looked older than they probably were. None of them looked like they smiled very much. I wondered if they were baseball fans.

I got hungry about three o'clock and went into a restaurant. It must've been one of the better places in town because there were men in suits and ties sitting at the tables. The ones facing the door stopped eating and stared at me when I walked in, stared so hard that the ones with their backs to the door finally turned around to see what it was. I stood there and looked at them all staring at me. My eyes moved from face to cold little face, and I can remember thinking: *God, so this is what it's like.* A woman was standing nearby with a couple of menus in her hand and she was staring at me too. So I went out.

I headed for the next place, which wasn't so fancy. It had a counter and a few crummy tables, but before I went in I saw some of the mountain boys sitting on stools with their backs to the counter, listening to the yokel music riproaring out of the jukebox. This isn't your spot either, man, I told myself.

I went to the bus terminal store. They had a coffee machine there and sold wrapped cake and doughnuts. I asked for a bus schedule and then bought some coffee and doughnuts and sat on the bench there and ate. There were some people sitting around with luggage, some of them black, and nobody paid me any attention. Well, I figured, I could at least eat coffee and doughnuts for two months. Nobody could blame me if I didn't hit .300 then.

Later, I collected my gear at the office, got a mummy's stare from Clidell Hapgood, and headed for the ballpark. It was about a mile outside of town. I walked along a black-topped road, me and my suitcase. There weren't many houses out there and I just walked along smelling the quiet air and listening to the birds singing in the trees. They sing for everybody, black and white alike. When I was a star in the big leagues I knew I was always going to remember this first walk out to the ballpark. I was lonely and scared and hungry and happy and proud, all of those things at the same time.

I saw the light towers showing over the trees. I'd never

31

played night ball and there was something real professional about it. Anybody could play ball during the day, but only the pros played at night. I loved the night games at Shea Stadium, the few times I was able to go.

Proctor Field wasn't Shea Stadium. You saw that right away. There was a wooden fence around the park and the bleachers weren't anywhere more than fifteen feet high. There were a few cars parked outside. I walked in past the empty ticket-taker's booth and here I was.

I went down a little runway and looked at the field. The grass looked a bit high in the outfield. The bleachers went only halfway down each line. There was a fellow making the left field foul line with a little wheel on a handle which he kept dipping into a bucket of whitewash. The batting cage was up. The fences looked to be pretty far out but I felt I could reach them.

The field lay under the late afternoon sunlight and I could smell the grass and it was all so very quiet. The way it should always be in the beginning.

Then I turned around and headed for the clubhouse. I figured it was time I met my teammates.

CHAPTER 5

The clubhouse was in a square whitewashed concrete building behind the stands. It had small, high windows. The door was open and as I headed for it I could hear voices inside. When I walked in, it all of a sudden got quiet. I stood in the doorway holding my suitcase and they looked at me and some of them dropped their eyes and looked at the floor. You can tell when you enter a room where everybody's been talking about you, by the way the quiet falls over.

Lloyd Rosewell was standing in the middle of the room, one foot up on a stool. I guess he'd been talking to them, telling them about me. I glanced over them all, one white face after the other. I was the only black one there.

"Johnny," Rosewell said when he saw me. "Come in."

He then introduced me to the team. Most of the fellows said Hi, a few just nodded, some didn't do anything. One or two sitting near stood up and shook hands. Rosewell then took me behind a screened-off area in another part of the room. That was his office. It had a desk and a chair. There was a cap and a pressed and ironed uniform folded up on the desk.

"This will be your suit, Johnny," he said. "Number nine."

"That's the number I had in high school," I said.

"When you're ready put it on and go out to the field and start working out. I'm playing you in left field tonight."

When I walked back into the dressing area some of the players had begun talking among themselves. None of them paid me much mind. They were starting to peel off their street clothes to get ready for the game.

There were no lockers. I had two nails on the wall to hang my things on. There was one long bench that we all shared. I sat down and started unlacing my shoes. I looked at the fellow next to me. He was a blond-haired guy. He was rubbing some leather oil into the pocket of his glove. Once in a while we looked at each other but didn't say anything.

Rosewell's voice came out from behind the screen: "Spence."

I stopped what I was doing and looked around. It turned out to be the guy sitting next to me. He was Spence. I knew something he didn't know—yet: they were releasing him. He put down his glove on the bench and got up and walked across the room. He was a tall, thin guy who walked like a cowboy. I felt real bad. For a minute I almost wished I hadn't come. You hate to turn somebody out of a job. I watched him go around into the office and then I looked down at his glove. It had a real good pocket, real professional.

Nobody said much to me. But I remembered how it was when a new kid came into class at school; nobody was too interested in him. He just had to work his way in. I supposed it was the same here.

There was some horseplay going on now. Somebody had soaked a roll of toilet paper in a bucket of water and now they were throwing it around. Then one of them picked up a bat and they pitched him the toilet paper and he rapped it across the clubhouse. It hit the far wall with a wet, dead noise.

"That's as far as he's hit anything all year," somebody yelled.

Then another fellow began to yell and curse. I watched him pull his foot slowly out of the spiked shoe he had just put on. He picked up the shoe and turned it over and egg yolk dripped out.

"Who did it?" he asked looking around.

Everybody laughed and I laughed too. He got a towel and wiped out the inside of his shoe and the bottom of his foot. Somebody yelled to him to keep his eggs in the refrigerator. When he asked again who did it somebody else told him it looked like the work of a chicken.

They took their time getting into their uniforms. One fellow was taping his ankle with white adhesive. Another was smoking a cigar and reading a sports magazine. Occasionally one glanced over at me but nobody said anything.

I saw Spence come out of the office and go straight to the john. You could tell from the way his shoulders were dropped forward that he'd been told. I seemed to be the only one thinking about it. He never came out of the john until the clubhouse was empty.

I smelled liniment. One guy was rubbing some on his arm. I figured him for a pitcher. Another guy was knocking dirt out of his cleats. Another one was sitting on a stool lightly swinging a bat back and forth. One guy was rolling a baseball up his arm and knocking it back into his hand with the point of his shoulder.

When I had pulled on my uniform I was dying to look into the mirror, but I didn't. I didn't think it would have been professional. Most of the players were suited up now. There was the sound of spikes on the concrete floor as they walked about. That was a most professional sound—spikes crackling on a concrete floor.

One by one the players headed for the field. Then I was alone in the clubhouse, except for Rosewell, who was in the office, and Spence, still in the john. I walked across the floor, listening to my spikes. Rosewell was sitting at the desk, in his uniform. He was filling in the line-up card.

"Mr. Rosewell?" I said.

"Call me Lloyd, Johnny."

"Yes sir. What should I do now?"

"Get out on the field and loosen up."

"Yes sir," I said.

When I passed the john I heard Spence in there blowing his nose.

There was nobody in the stands yet. The visiting team wasn't on the field, just the Proctor players. One group was playing pepper, some others were having a game of catch, while a few were sitting in the dugout. There were only eighteen on the team; that's what they carry in the low minors. They want to give everybody the chance to play.

I wandered up to the fellows playing catch and stood there. They were lobbing the ball back and forth. I wondered if they were going to throw it to me. It came into my head that they were not going to throw it to me, that they would try to freeze me out.

Have dignity, man, I told myself. Don't say anything. Just wait it out. I watched the ball loop through the air. They were going in rotation, one across to the other. Then it was my turn. I was so sure I wasn't going to get the toss that I almost got hit in the head with it when it did come to me, so surprised I was. The ball flopped into my glove and I put my fingers around it and so help me didn't want to throw it back. It was a professional baseball and I wanted to squeeze it and look at it and smell it. I felt as if all of the game's heart was inside that ball, beating soft and warm. I held it tender in my hand, like it was a newborn chick. Then I had to laugh to myself as I tossed it back: two hours later I was going to be trying to hit a professional baseball as sharp and far as I could.

When batting practice started I went to the outfield to shag fly balls. I tried to look nonchalant and dropped one. That ended nonchalant. When it started to get dark they put the lights on. The lights didn't bring daylight the way they did at Shea Stadium, but were pretty weak, especially in the outfield. The outfield wasn't big league either; the grass was high, and here and there was broken glass.

Then I heard Lloyd calling me in to hit. I ran down

37

the left field line to the batting cage. I hefted a few bats, found my style, and stepped into the cage.

"Five licks, normally," Lloyd said from behind the cage. "But tonight you take ten."

The pitcher was throwing mostly for control. He threw five fast balls before he bent one. He was throwing pretty lively and got the first two right by me until I had gauged him. Then I got wood on one and popped it over second base. He was right-handed and I swing left, so I had the advantage. I hit a few line drives into right-center and that made me feel better. There's nothing like smacking a baseball right on the button to pick you up. I smelled out when he was going to his curve and timed it just right and banged it way out to right field. It might have been going over but I didn't watch it; you don't do that in batting practice, as a rule. I always went to the big league games early, to watch the pre-game stuff, and I studied those boys in the batting cage. One day I saw Willie hit three in a row into the left field chairs and never look up once.

After I'd taken my rips I went back to the clubhouse. I was nervous, I guess, and was heading for the john. The place was empty, except for Spence. I'd forgot about him. He was sitting there in his street clothes, his bag at his feet. The bag was unzipped and he was just putting his glove in. He looked up at me when I came in.

"I was it," he said. He had a little smile, a hurt smile.

"Pardon me?" I said.

"They had to let somebody go when you came on, and I was it."

"I'm sorry," I said.

He shrugged.

38

"Somebody had to go," he said. "I knew it was going to be me."

"You an outfielder?"

"Yeah."

"What were you hitting?" I asked.

"Two twenty-two."

I was sorry I asked. It was like asking a pauper to give you his financial report.

"Is the league tough?" I asked. But that was dumb too. Of course it was tough—for him. He didn't answer.

"Maybe you'll be able to hook up someplace else."

"I'm going to try," he said. "Lloyd said he was going to make some phone calls."

"I wish you luck, man," I said.

He nodded. "Good luck to you," he said. Then he looked down and said, like he was talking to the bag, "I'm going to tell them back home that I hurt my shoulder and couldn't swing the bat. I reckon that's what I'm going to tell them."

When I went back to the field the visiting team had begun to make their appearance. They had Eden Forest on their uniforms, which was the name of the town they were from. Some people were in the stands now. A loud-speaker was playing hillbilly music while the Eden Forest team worked out. I sat in the dugout, holding my glove. Most of the Proctor players had gone back to the clubhouse to dry off after the pre-game workout. I was sitting there alone, watching the Eden Forest players take batting practice. I didn't see any blacks on that team either.

Well, by game time there must've been three or four hundred people in the stands, more than I had ever played in front of before. When the P.A. system said my name in the line-up I was so startled I turned around. Lloyd had put me second on the card so I was right out there on deck when the first man went up. He went out on the first pitch and there I was, stepping into professional baseball.

I tried to stand in there very calm and quiet and serious. The important thing was to look professional. I pumped the bat back and forth a few times, then drew it back and set it as the pitcher swung into his windup.

The first pitch I saw was a fast ball right down the pipe. I was so scared I didn't swing; I couldn't swing. The bat suddenly felt like it weighed fifty pounds. I stepped out for a second and rubbed some dirt on my hands and gave myself a talking. *You swing that bat, man, and you hit that ball.* That's what I told myself.

The pitcher was a chunky right-hander who threw hard. Most young pitchers in the minors throw hard. That's how they get signed. You don't see many young pitchers who throw cute. He took his sign in a crouch and went right to work, all business. He gave me another fast ball which moved away and sank and I hit it to the shortstop on one bounce. He threw me out.

My next time up I ran the count to three and one, then swung at a bad pitch and got a single up the middle. When the ball went through some of the guys yelled at me and clapped their hands. It made me feel real good.

But what I remember most from that first game is coming up in the sixth inning with a man on first. We were on the tail end of a 2–1 score. Working out of a stretch, the pitcher got two strikes on me. Then he tried to jam me with a fast ball but got the pitch out just a bit too far and I jumped on it. I got under it and hit it hard. The ball rose fast and as I ran down the line I knew I had hit a ball as hard as I could. I watched the right-fielder. He was running back, his glove hand raised high. *Go out*, I was thinking, talking to the ball. And then I saw him stop, just as I was buzzing around first base, and let his arms drop to his sides. He was looking at the fence, his back to the field. The ball was gone. A home run.

I'll never forget that trot around the bases. Some people were cheering and clapping their hands. The pitcher was standing on the mound with his hands on his hips, looking at the ground. I kept my head down, my face plain, even though inside of me everything was trying to stretch my face into a smile and push me into a dance. As I came around third I heard a voice come out of the stands, good and loud:

"Hey, coon, pretty good."

I think we won the game.

CHAPTER 6

There was a certain routine that they followed after a home game. After they had showered and got dressed, they piled into a couple of cars that belonged to the players and drove back to town. There was a side-street restaurant called Latimer's that always stayed open for them and they went there to eat.

I'd showered fast and got dressed ahead of anybody else and was standing in front of the clubhouse when they started to come out. A few of them went by without saying anything, but then the third baseman, a big guy named Walt Peterson, asked me if I wanted to come with them for a bite to eat. He didn't have to ask twice.

Latimer's had a counter and a half dozen tables with cloths on them. Usually, by the time the team got there they were the only customers. About ten of us, which was more than half the team, went there that night. We ordered hamburgers and Cokes and french fries and malted milks.

Latimer didn't seem to mind my being there. He was

a quiet cat who nodded his head up and down in little spurts when you talked to him, but who seldom answered. Peterson introduced me to him and Latimer said he was happy to meet me. We shook hands, too. I was beginning to notice those things—who shook hands with me and who didn't.

I dropped a quarter into the juke box, just to be a good guy, and pressed the names of songs and artists I'd never heard of. It was country music, played with a twangy band and sung by people whose big grinning white teeth you could see just by listening.

Some of the guys mixed with me and I got the feeling they were doing it because they felt like it, not because they were trying to be nice or do me a favor or make themselves feel better. The ones who didn't talk much to me were guys who didn't seem to talk much to anybody, who just seemed to be naturally quiet.

Curfew was midnight and by eleven-thirty some of the guys began to drift out. The catcher, a stubby guy from Cleveland named Squalls, came over to me.

"Where you living, Johnny?" he asked.

Well, I'd forgot about that. Lloyd had said it would be taken care of, but he had left straight after the game. So here I was, facing a second night in Proctor without a place to bunk.

"I don't have a place yet," I said.

"No?" he said. "What do you do then?"

I shrugged.

"I'd ask you to room with us tonight," he said, "but the landlord is anti-Negro."

"That's surprising, isn't it?" I said it with a straight

face and he looked at me puzzled for a second, then started to laugh.

Then he said, "So what are you gonna do?"

"Patrol," I said.

"Patrol what?"

"The streets, man. Maybe I'll sleep in the park. Is there a park in this town?"

"Behind the movie theater. There's some benches."

One of the pitchers, Bill Savage, had been listening in. Now he said:

"Let's sneak him in."

He was Squalls' roomie. They looked at each other and started to laugh. They liked the idea. I didn't.

When we left Latimer's I was walking in the middle and they were trying to talk me into what sounded like a bad idea.

"You can't sleep on a park bench," Squalls said. "It ain't dignified."

"You might get a sore back," Savage said.

"You could get arrested."

"It might rain."

I kept telling them no, that I didn't want to make any trouble for anybody. I made up stories about having slept in parks before, about what a hard fellow I was, and what a tough life I had led. The truth was I was one tired and bone-weary colored boy. I hadn't slept on the bus coming down and the jail cot had been like sleeping on a pool table. You needed your rest if you wanted to play a good game of baseball, and, man, I wanted more than anything in the world to play a good game.

Next thing I knew we were standing in front of their rooming house. There was an upstairs and a downstairs,

44

with one light shining on each floor. There were some big old heavy trees standing cover on each side of the house.

"How do I get out in the morning?" I asked.

"We sleep later than anybody else," Squalls said. "They've all gone to work by the time we get up."

"How about the lady of the house?"

"We'll slip you past her in the morning," Savage said. He was a big tall guy with blond hair that was chopped down to a brush. He was from someplace west, like Colorado or Wyoming, I forget where.

So I followed them to the door, still carrying the suitcase. We tiptoed up the porch steps, Squalls going first, then Savage, then me. Squalls went in, had a look around inside, then came back to the door and put one finger to his lips and waved us on with his other hand. He looked like a third base coach waving in a runner in slow motion.

I followed Savage into the house. There was a room next to the staircase and I could hear a television set going. If Savage hadn't had his hand on my arm I might've turned around and bucked out at that second. But then Squalls had passed the room and was waving again, again in slow motion, from the foot of the stairs.

I put my head down and hurried past the room. There was a thick old carpet going up the staircase and we didn't make any noise walking up. At the head of the stairs, hanging on the wall, was a big knitted thing that said "God Bless Us All."

There were three or four doors upstairs. Squalls opened theirs and we started to go in. Just as we were closing the door the one on the opposite side of the hall opened and I caught just a glimpse of a guy coming out,

45

tall and bony, wearing a bathrobe. I didn't think he saw me, our door was just about going shut when his opened. He had a towel over his arm and a bar of soap in his hand and he seemed to me to have been looking down.

After the door was shut Savage stood with his back against it and went, "Whew!"

"You think he saw me?" I whispered.

"No, don't worry," Squalls said.

It was a nice-sized room, with two beds and a sofa. To me it looked like the Waldorf Astoria after the last two nights.

"You can grab the sofa," Squalls said to me.

I would have done that, too. I would have done it and been asleep in thirty seconds. But we heard voices in the hall at that moment, busy voices, like the talkers were in a hurry. Then the voices were outside the door, then somebody was knocking.

"Mr. Squalls? Mr. Savage?" It was a woman's voice. We all looked at each other.

"Yes, Mrs. Terry?" Squalls said.

"Do you have someone in there?" the woman asked.

We still looked at each other. Then I looked at the window.

"Do we have someone in here?" Squalls said.

"Mr. Henshaw said he saw someone in there," the woman said. Then her voice got lower, but not softer; harder, if anything. "A colored person."

"A colored person?" Squalls said.

I was at the window now. It was open. There was a little roof—from the porch—slanting down.

"Yes," the woman said.

"Ask her what color," Savage whispered.

46

"A colored person?" Squalls said again.

"Yes," the woman said again.

"Mr. Henshaw said that?" Squalls said.

I moved my suitcase out first, then climbed over the window sill onto the roof. I got to the edge and looked down. It was about a ten-foot drop. I could hear them talking. It was Squalls.

"You can't come in just now," he was saying. "Mr. Savage is naked."

I had two hopes at the moment: that the suitcase wouldn't make too much noise when it landed, and that I wouldn't break an ankle. If I did, I would tell the boys back home that it had happened sliding into third trying to stretch a double. That would be my story. Trying to outrun the peg from right field I hit the dirt and my spikes caught and . . .

The suitcase didn't make too much noise. Then I was hanging from the edge of the porch, not wanting to let go. I could hear the woman's voice clear now; she was in the room. I could hear Savage making a fuss, about invasion of privacy, and taking this to the Chamber of Commerce. My fingers were getting tired, but I didn't want to let go. So I let go not wanting to and hit the ground and tumbled backwards and landed on the soft earth of Virginia, in the Blue Ridge Mountains. When I realized that I hadn't broken anything I jumped up, grabbed my suitcase, and took off.

I slipped out of the front gate and hurried off into the night. I went to the park behind the movie house and slept on a bench. There were a lot of mosquitoes. And they didn't discriminate against me, either.

CHAPTER 7

"A park bench?" Lloyd said. "Well, I'm sorry. I meant to . . . last night. But we'll see to it right now."

He was sitting in the kitchen of his rooming house, eating breakfast. I was standing there holding my suitcase, hoping somebody would ask me to breakfast. But nobody did. I was hungry again. It seemed that ever since coming to Proctor I'd been either looking for a place to sleep or been hungry, and most of the time both.

We left the house and got into Lloyd's car and drove off. We drove into the outskirts of town, which happened pretty quick. I mean, you went only a couple of blocks and you were in the outskirts of Proctor.

He pulled up in front of a dead-looking shebang of a house located on a dirt road off the main drag. It was a one-level job and looked to have had additions built onto it, starting with the Civil War—the place looked that old. It stood off by itself, surrounded by empty rocky ground and a few old trees.

Lloyd pumped the horn a couple times. The front door opened and an old black lady came out, walked across the front porch, which was ground level, and came toward us.

"That's Mrs. Wilson," Lloyd said. "She's a nice old lady."

She looked in the window, first at me, then at Lloyd. She was about sixty, gray, with a tired face. She talked slow.

"This here is Johnny Lee, Mrs. Wilson," Lloyd said. "He's looking for a place to stay."

She looked me over now.

"How long you been in town, boy?" she asked.

"Two days," I said.

"I'll rent you a room," she said. Which meant she knew I'd tried the other places—the better places—and here I was.

I had a room on the side of the house, with my own entrance. It had a bed and a table and two chairs and a small chest of drawers. The Wilsons charged me twenty dollars a week, which included meals. They had six children who all were grown up and married and scattered around the country. I guess they were lonely now and took in stray cats like me from time to time.

Mr. Wilson was an old-timer, thin as a rail, with little patches of gray hair curled up here and there around the sides and back of his head. He was night watchman in a lumber yard, which meant he was around during the day.

I was sitting on a chair outside of my room later that day, listening to my transistor, when he came by. He had a friendly, smiley face. He pulled up an old wooden milk crate and sat on it.

"You're not the first one they had," he said.

"First what?" I asked.

"They had a boy named Langdon a couple, three years ago. He lived here too. I'd hear him crying at night sometimes, or find him sitting out here in the afternoon staring at the ground in such a way you'd thought he was trying to drill holes there with his eyes. He was a northern boy, just like you. Boston, or Illinois, or some such place. He just wasn't used to things down here."

"What happened to him?"

"He was more sensitive than most," Mr. Wilson said. "Some people take things to heart more easy than others. That's what happened to him. You might as well make up your mind they're not gonna like you. So you got to make 'em respect you. That's the most to hope for and that's a lot."

"What happened to him?" I asked.

"He come here in May. Ever body said he was good, too."

"How long did he stay?"

"Four weeks."

"He should've stuck it out," I said. "You've got to stick it out."

"You been here how long now?"

"Two days."

He took a cold pipe out of his shirt pocket and put it in his mouth and nodded his head. Then he shifted his eyes to my face and gave me a sad little smile.

Lloyd had me at the ballpark that afternoon at one o'clock. He said he didn't like the way I charged ground balls. He was hoping to play me in center field and to do that I was going to have to be a much better outfielder than I was. He wanted me to come in faster on the grounders and scoop them up like an infielder. Otherwise, he said, runners would be taking an extra base on me. It was true I was slow coming in on those balls, but I had a good arm and I figured that made up for it. I told him so, too.

"Bull," he said. "This is pro ball. You'll find the base runners are faster and smarter. You lay back and I don't care how good your arm is, they'll run on you. And unless you lay that ball on the dime every time, they're going to beat you."

It was a hot day, up in the nineties, with no breeze. He had me out there for two hours, steady. He stood at home plate knocking them out to me, line drives that landed short and that I had to keep charging in for. I tried not to miss a one, to show him I was better than he thought I was. Coming in at top speed I did miss a few. After a while he yelled out to me that I was coming in *too* fast (after I'd overrun a couple).

By three o'clock I was soaking wet and hot and tired. But I said to myself, *Hell, I'm going to stay out here all day and all night too if he asks for it.* If he thought he was going to use up all the kick I had in me he had another think coming. I kept charging those balls and picking them up and whipping them in to the kid he had standing there catching for him, and he kept whacking them right back out to me, grounders and line drives.

After a while I could feel the sun starting to make me dizzy. The inside of my head felt like it was being filled with cotton and I had to shake it and blink my eyes to beat off the feeling. I started to think about Langdon. I didn't know who he was and what problems he might have had. I only knew I was Johnny Lee, I had come there to play professional baseball, and nobody was going to make me pack my bag and quit. Toward the end of the workout I was so tired I had to tell my body when to move and my brain what to do, instead of doing it all natural, on instinct. *Here it comes, man, run in, fast, get your glove down, pick up that ball clean, fire it.* Over and over and over. I could feel the sweat rolling down my throat and chest. I would've given anything for a swallow of water, but I wasn't going to give him the satisfaction. *I'm tougher than Langdon,* I started to think. *I'm tougher than Langdon.*

Lloyd seemed to be getting smaller, and farther away, like he was dropping down the far end of a telescope. The bleachers looked to be swaying around behind him, like they were under water. You're getting sunstroke, boy, I told myself. I even looked up at the sky a few times, as if to tell the sun to stop stroking me, that I wasn't going to quit. I'm tougher than Langdon, I said to the sun, out loud. Standing out there in center field talking to myself. I was really starting to blow my mind.

Then he was waving me in. I ran in, too, right across the infield, fast as I could, even though my legs were saying, *You're crazy, man.* He didn't say anything when I passed him. I went to the clubhouse and straight to the john. I closed the door behind me and stood there. My heart was beating like a drum. I was hot and dizzy and sweated. Suddenly I threw up the lunch Mrs. Wilson had made for me.

I was sitting on the clubhouse bench fanning myself when Lloyd came in. He told me to be back in two hours. The bus left from the park at five o'clock sharp, he said.

"The bus?" I said.

"We're playing in Gilmore tonight," he said.

CHAPTER 8

The bus was yellow, with the name of the team painted in blue on both sides. It had a rattle in back and had a hard time going up hills. The seats were covered with a stiff black leather and crunched whenever you shifted around in them. We did all of our traveling in this bus, and some of the trips were three or four hours. Coming home was the worst, because you were tired after the game and had to sleep as best you could on those seats.

We never went away for overnight. No matter how far away we played we always came back the same night. In some of the towns we played in the visiting club didn't have a shower in the dressing room and so we had to ride back all sweaty and grimy. If we had lost the game the ride back was pretty stiff. You weren't supposed to laugh or crack jokes or sing because it wouldn't look professional. If we won the game, then it was different.

An old man who owned the bus always drove us. He never said hello to me the whole summer. Lloyd sat up front and nobody was allowed to sit next to him unless asked to. Sometimes he asked the starting pitcher to sit with him awhile.

If you were able to sleep on the bus you were lucky. Otherwise you just had to sit there and look at the trees go by. I was one who couldn't sleep on the bus. I was always excited, going to the game, wondering what was going to happen, and then coming back, thinking about what had happened. Some of the guys brought pillows and blankets with them and stretched out on the floor and went to sleep there. There sure wasn't much to see from the window, a farmhouse now and then with a light on, that was about all.

I was real tired going out that first night. I'd gone back to my place and taken a shower, then borrowed a rusty old bike from the Wilsons and pedaled out to the ballpark, with my gear in a wire basket attached to the handlebars. When everybody had shown up we took off.

Most of the guys on the team were pretty friendly. Squalls and Savage were the friendliest. They told me that Gilmore was a pretty rough town. Of all the towns in the league, this one was in the deadest nowhere. They had a lot of hillbillies coming to the games and the hillbillies were real rough on the visiting teams. They'd yell a lot and sometimes throw things. I got the message, even though it wasn't said straight out.

On top of everything else, Gilmore was leading the league. They had the best pitchers and the two leading hitters as well as the top home run hitter. We were in fifth place at the moment, twelve games out of first.

I was taking my batting practice cuts when the first people started coming into the stands. They spotted me right off and began to yell at me. I knew all the words, it was just that I had never heard them directed to me like that, out loud and in public. Squalls told me not to listen to them, but that would have been a good trick. In a park that small, with the stands so close and the crowd so small, you can hear everything. It made me burn up inside. But I didn't show anything.

While I was sitting on the bench just before the start of the game I was almost hoping I wouldn't have such a good night, so as not to stir up those hillbillies. They were real nasty. I could see them sitting behind the Gilmore dugout drinking beer and yelling and having a high old time for themselves. The visiting club didn't have a dugout, we sat out in the open on a bench, so you never had the chance to get away from them.

Gilmore started a left-hander named Harrison. He was about six-four and stringy. He brought that left arm around from first base and threw the ball harder than anybody I had ever seen. (He was 11–1 on the year so far.) He had a long, slow windup, and when his hands got over his head he raised his knee way above his middle and then pivoted and fired. The ball came in like a bullet and looked about as big.

Our leadoff man struck out on three pitches. Then I stepped in. The yelling got real loud and unfriendly, but most of it I truly didn't hear because I was concentrating so hard on that pitcher. I set myself back in the box, took a few practice chops, and brought the bat back, raised it, and set it high behind my left ear.

I watched him take his sign, sweep low, raise that knee, and then let go. Well, I suppose I should have expected it. I think I knew it a split second before he let go of the ball, but even then it was too late. A beanball is right on top of you, right away, and then seems to hang there for just that moment, showing itself off to you. That's the only time I really saw it, and I had just that moment to get out of the way. I moved so fast that my cap stayed where my head had been and Squalls told me later that the ball went between my empty cap and my head.

I went down so fast I never had time to let go of the bat and I lay on the ground still holding it over my shoulder. Then I got up, picked up my cap, put it on, and stepped back in. (I had forgotten to put on my batting helmet but I was damned if I was going to ask for it now.) I didn't even dust my trousers. My heart was beating like I'd just played two hours of basketball and I was scared—not from what had happened but what had almost happened. That ball would've gone right through my head, man, and come out the other side.

I tried not to look scared. The hillbillies were yelling and some of the Gilmore players were yelling too.

"That's looking them over, black boy!" was one of the things I heard.

Harrison, the pitcher, never blinked an eye. He had long sideburns and a long, hang-jaw face. He just stood there waiting for his sign.

"Hang loose, kid," I heard the catcher say behind me.

Loose. I was so loose that a good strong breeze would've picked me up. But I made a big show of planting my spikes and crowding the plate.

Harrison picked up his sign and wound up again. He

brought up that knee, reared back and fired, over the plate this time. I swung late and tapped it down to third. I was thrown out on a close play.

When I got back to the bench our pitcher, Leo Koronski, a tough Polish guy from Milwaukee, looked at me and said:

"That's hanging in there." Those were the first words he'd spoken to me.

Then, in the second inning, I knew I was on the team. I was standing out in left field. The first Gilmore batter came up. I watched Koronski wind up and the next thing I knew the Gilmore guy was flat on his back. Koronski had decked him, to get even. I knew just why he had done it, too. It wasn't because *I* had been thrown at, but because a *teammate* had been decked that Koronski did it. And I liked it better that way. Nobody was thrown at after that, on either side.

It became a tight ballgame. I forgot how tired I was. We went into the ninth tied at 1–1. I led off. Harrison wasn't throwing as hard now as he had been in the beginning. He came in with a fast ball and I got around on it and pulled it on a line over the first baseman's head. I got two bases out of it. The next man bunted me over and I scored on a long fly to right by Peterson. We won it 2–1. I caught the last out in left field, and when I went running in with the ball I heard a big fat round voice yell out, "You lousy nigger." I guess he was talking to me.

It was a great ride back. We sang for an hour straight. It was the first time all season they'd won from Gilmore. In spite of all, the afternoon workout and everything, I was full of pep when we got back to Proctor. Latimer's was still open—he waited for us sometimes—and we went in for a feed. After that all of the fellows split up into groups and went back to their rooming houses, to sit around and bull or play cards.

I walked home alone to the Wilsons'.

CHAPTER 9

I called home after a few days to talk to my folks. My Pa asked me how I was doing.

"I'm still here," I said.

"We're rooting for you, Johnny," he said.

"I'm sending you a newspaper clipping," I said. "You save them, you hear?"

The day after the Gilmore game I got a little write-up in the one and only Proctor paper. It said I was built like a "whippet." It said I was a wrist hitter who hit the ball with power, ran with terrific speed, covered my position well, and had an arm like a cannon. That's what it said in the paper. I bought copies of the paper and sent the clipping to all my friends. I bought so many papers that the man must have thought I was going into business for myself.

I couldn't wait to play ball every night. On purpose I slept as late as I could every day, just to make the waiting time till the game that much shorter. The afternoons were pretty empty. I either sat outside the Wilsons' house and played my transistor or else walked around town and looked in the windows. I didn't pal around with the other players too much, even though I liked some of them a lot and knew that some of them liked me. You just didn't see it—black and white guys walking together as friends, jiving each other.

I went into Latimer's in the afternoon for coffee and a sandwich and found some of the guys there. We would sit around and jive each other. That was our hangout.

If a home game got rained out we'd go to the movies together, then to Latimer's, but that was about it. I never went to any of their houses, though now and then Squalls or Savage would show up at the Wilsons' and we'd sit around and talk baseball.

The team got going real good after I came in. We ripped off a nine-game win streak and started to move up in the standings. After the first two weeks I was hitting .350.

I still hated going on the road to some of those towns. There were only four or five other black players in the league. Sometimes we'd get together before a game and talk about our problems. It was always the same—the loneliness, the having to be apart from so much. It could be rough on the field, too. In a town like Gilmore the crowd was dead set against the black players. One guy told me that when he got spiked there and was being helped off the field some of the hillbillies stood up and started to sing "Old Black Joe" at him.

And there were a lot of pitchers who were still trying to throw that ball through my head. I went down a lot and got hit a few times. One guy pinked me on the wrist and almost broke it. Another guy put a fast ball in my ribs and I felt tears come to my eyes, the pain was so bad.

One night there was some heat in Mariontown during one of our games. I was trying to score from second on a single and slid hard into home. My foot kicked the ball out of the catcher's glove and I was safe. I hadn't done it on purpose but the next thing I knew the catcher was cursing me and throwing his glove into my face. I threw it back at him and jumped up and we would've gone at each other except the umpire stepped in. He pushed me back and he had the wildest look in his eye, like I was crazy. Then a lot of players came out and broke it up.

When I walked back to our bench I saw all the people standing up and yelling at me and shaking their fists. Then they started throwing stuff, beer cans and paper and lit cigarettes and whatever else they could pick up. Lloyd looked down the bench at me and said:

"I'm taking you out of the game. Go to the clubhouse —and lock the door."

"Why?" I asked.

He got mad. "I'm telling you to go to the clubhouse!" he yelled.

I took my glove and did like he said. The fans were really screaming and maybe I was glad to duck in there and lock the door. Later, after the game, Lloyd came in and he was still teed off.

"What the hell did you do that for?" he asked.

"Do what?" I asked.

"Were you trying to start a riot?"

"He threw his glove at me."

"I don't care what he threw," he said.

I could see he was mad, so I buttoned up. A few

nights earlier almost the same exact thing had happened. Somebody had come in hard to Jimmy Squalls trying to score and Squalls had got up and punched the guy out. But that was all right. Everybody was allowed to fight back except me.

"Everybody except me," I said to Squalls on the bus back that night.

"Sure," he said, laughing. "We don't want our .350 hitter to get hurt."

"That ain't the reason, man," I said. I was still sore.

The next day I told the story to old Mr. Wilson. He just smiled.

"Maybe where you come from," he said, "things have changed. But not here. No sir, I don't see no change. I can go up to the highest mountain in the range and look with the biggest telescope, and I won't see no change."

"The change will come," I said. "If it doesn't come around those mountains or across them, then it'll come *through*, like a bulldozer."

"You're so sure it will?"

"I know it," I said.

"Then you have something on them, if you're so sure."

"What do you mean?"

"Get in the car," he said.

He had a car that was way older than I was. We got in and drove off. The car rattled and shook and coughed and sneezed, but somehow it got him where he wanted to go; probably because he never wanted to go anywheres he shouldn't.

We drove out of town. After going a few miles he turned up a dirt road and began climbing into the

63

mountains. After going about a mile or so he stopped.

We were in the middle of nowhere. The land was flat and grassy on one side of the road; wooded on the other. We got out of the car. Mr. Wilson lit his pipe and began walking through the grass. He was bent over just a little. He always kept one hand in the pocket of his windbreaker when he walked, the pipe in the other.

"This heah," he said, "used to be one grand piece of land. It was owned by the Richardson family, going back before the War Between the States. The Richardsons were the biggest, the most powerfulest, and the richest family in Proctor County. My grandfather was one of their slaves. He was a boy maybe your age then, when this happened. He lived to be God knows how old and I knew him a little before he died. He told me this story. He brought me up here one day and told me.

"This happened just before the war. The Richardsons had a son, a wild, spoiled, headstrong chap named Andrew. The old man said he was very unkind, that sometimes he beat the slaves. One day my grandfather was out heah clearing off some rocks, loading them onto a wagon, when he saw Andrew come riding across the grass.

"He was one fine rider, the old man said. But this day his luck was not so good. There used to be a rail fence up against those trees. The old man said Andrew tried to jump it and ride on the other side—the trees weren't so big then, of course.

"But he—Andrew—never made it. The horse threw him as it went over. He hit the ground like a rock, the old man said. The horse kept going. Being a good slave, my grandfather ran over to help. But when he got there he saw Andrew lying in the bushes, dead, his neck broke. The young master was dead. The pride of the whole clan was dead. Then my grandfather looked up, he said, and watched the horse running away. He decided right then and there what he was going to do.

"What did he do? I'll tell you what he did, Johnny. He did naught. He went on about his business. At sundown he brought his mule and wagon back to the overseer's cabin. That night he bedded down in the slave quarters and didn't say anything to anybody, not to his mother or his father or his brothers or his sisters.

"Naturally, the next day there was a whole lot of excitement going on. The young master's horse had been found with the saddle empty. The slaves knew ever thing, of course. They knew all that went on in the grand house, because they weren't supposed to know anything. Oh, they knew a lot of things.

"Days passed and ever body was searching for the young master. They looked ever where. They combed here and there. But they never found him. Not even the slaves knew what had happened to him—none except the boy, my grandfather. He held his secret. About six months after, he had occasion to come back to this place, where we're standing now. He went and had a look and sure enough, it was still there, turning to skeleton now, lying in the bushes, mostly covered. After about a year passed he looked again. All that was there now was mostly the old finery, and the boots. And he held his secret. He never told a soul till years later he told me."

"Why?" I asked when Mr. Wilson had stopped talking.

Mr. Wilson lit his pipe, smiling into his cupped hands as he puffed away. He shook out the match and threw it down. He looked up and breathed the sweet air, a secret little smile on his lips.

"Why?" he asked. I knew he was going to say that. He was that kind of old philosopher who would answer Why with Why.

"Why didn't he ever tell them?" I asked. "Was he scared?"

"No, he wasn't scared. He had nothing to be scared about. But by not telling, by knowing they were wondering and would always wonder—remember now, he was a slave—he knew that *he* had something on *them*. That was his strength. He knew something big and mighty that they didn't. He said that helped him see through his days and nights of being—how do you say it—down-pressed? He knew something that they didn't. Just like you say that you know for sure, danged almighty sure, that the change is coming and that these people heah don't know it. That's *your* strength, boy. Come on now. Let's go back."

CHAPTER 10

A couple of days after the brawl, or near brawl, I had with that catcher in Mariontown, Lloyd had me out to the field for another afternoon workout. This time he had me chasing fungoes. He stood at home plate and rapped long, high fly balls all over the park and set me to chasing them. He said I wasn't getting the proper jump on the ball and that I wasn't going back correctly on balls hit over my head, that sometimes I turned the wrong way.

It was another of those hot days. The summer had really set in. No matter where you went, in the shade or under a tree, it was July. This place was like the main oven where they baked all the Julys.

I had never had trouble on fly balls before (it was true that I got a bad jump on one the other night and it dropped in front of me and cost two runs). There weren't many that went over my head. Why, Lloyd himself had moved me over to center field and I was doing the job real fine.

So again I stood out there in that heat and chased baseballs. This time it was for just an hour. Then he brought me in for some batting practice. He had rounded up a bunch of kids and given them a few bucks and now one of them, a high school boy, pitched to me while the others spread out in the outfield. The kid had a pretty decent curve but not much speed, so I didn't see what good this could do me. I felt pretty silly, too, taking batting practice. My average at the moment was .345, highest on the team. (Lloyd himself was hitting but .305.) I didn't see any of the .250 hitters out there. I was the only one.

Lloyd stood behind the cage and watched me take my rips. I hit a lot of hard line drives and sent a few balls over the fence; I was pretty mad. He never said anything when I sent a ball blistering; the only time he said anything was to criticize. He told me my stride was wrong, my swing too sweeping.

"Cut down on that swing," he said. "Tighten it up."

My hands were beginning to hurt. I didn't say anything. I stayed mad and kept ripping the ball.

He kept me in the cage for two hours. It was finally the kid pitchers—he rotated three of them—who began to drag their tails, so we stopped. When I went to the clubhouse my hands were real tender. I was afraid of raising blisters. That would sit me down. The idea of that got me uptight and when Lloyd walked in, pulling his sweatshirt up over his head, I said:

"Lloyd, what's the reason for all this? You've got guys hitting .250."

When the sweatshirt cleared his face I saw he was

mad. He pulled the shirt free and threw it down on the bench.

"Dammit," he said, "sure they're hitting .250 and they're going to keep hitting .250 as long as they live. Don't think you're such a hotshot because you're hitting the ball in this league. What do you think the pitching's like in the next classification, and the one over that?"

He paced around the clubhouse, his spikes clacking on the floor. The perspiration was running down his chest and back.

"I'll tell you something," he said. "There isn't a pitcher in this league who knows how to change speeds properly. You move up and you're going to find them. So if you keep overstriding and taking that big swing you're going to find yourself off balance all the time. Pitchers are pretty smart you know. They can figure things out. Maybe not in this league so much."

He paced around some more, toweling himself.

"You think you were born to hit .350?" he asked. "Nobody is. Nobody has a God-given right to hit .350— not Williams, not Musial, not anybody. You want to make it in baseball you have to work your tail off, keep improving. You have the talent—you have the capacity to improve. That's why I'm working with you. If you don't want to do it, if you don't have the stomach, just tell me."

He walked to his office, big, bare-chested. Suddenly he turned around.

"Do you think I enjoy standing out there in the sun?" He started for the office again, then turned around once more. "And don't tell me how to manage." Then he went into the office.

That night, in the game, I followed some of the things he told me. I got two triples and a single.

A few days later I found a lot of excitement when I got to the ballpark. Squalls came up to me and said:

"Do you know who's here?" He didn't even give me the chance to say that I didn't know. "Walt Bonninger."

"What's he doing here?" I asked.

"He's come to watch us play."

Walt Bonninger was from the front office of the big club. He was chief scout. He was making a swing of all the farm clubs. He would do that once or twice each season, to check up on the players, to do a little scouting of his own. This was one of the men you had to impress if you wanted to get anywhere.

Everybody was real nervous. I'd never seen the clubhouse so quiet. Savage was pitching that night and he sat off in a corner by himself just staring into space. We were playing Gilmore. They were still in first place but we were making a run at them now. We were just five games in back of them, in third place. But they were still a very tough team.

When I got out on the field I saw the fellow who had to be Walt Bonninger. He was sitting behind our dugout with Clidell Hapgood, who seemed never to stop talking. Clidell was the type who buttered up anybody he thought was better than him (that took in the whole rest of the world, as far as I was concerned). I could see him jawing away, pointing out one thing and another.

"He's saying how beautiful the lights are," Squalls said.

"No," somebody else said, "he's telling how they've got the outfield grass down to ten inches now."

Bonninger was just nodding to all of Clidell's talk. He was a big man and was wearing sun glasses. All of the guys were trying to look at him without appearing that they were, like out of the corners of their eyes. The pre-game workout was most serious and snappy.

The game was a disaster. Everybody tried too hard. Savage lasted two innings. I could tell right off, from where I stood in center field, that he wasn't pitching with his natural motion. He was trying so hard that he made himself tense. He was wild with his fast ball and his curve was flat. Nobody else did much better, including me. I wanted Bonninger to see I could hit long home runs. I figured he'd take me back with him that night and send me right on up to the big leagues. I didn't get the ball out of the infield in four swings.

Later, after the game, when I was getting dressed, Lloyd came over to me and said:

"Mr. Bonninger wants to see you outside."

I got dressed as fast as I could, trying to figure out what it could be. But you can never figure out what a big shot is going to say. If you could, then you would be the big shot and he would be you.

When I went outside he was sitting in the grand-stand behind the dugout, alone. The only light still on was behind home plate. The outfield was all covered up with darkness. It all looked kind of spooky.

I walked around to the front of the grandstand and stood there and looked at him for a second. He still had on the dark glasses. He was a big man, huge around the shoulders, and his arms filled out the sleeves of his polo shirt.

"I'm Johnny Lee," I said.

"Sit down, Johnny," he said.

I came up there and plunked down next to him.

"Bad game," I said. "Everybody had a bad game. They were nervous. Me too. We were all nervous. It would be better if you could sneak into town and nobody know you're watching."

"I didn't think it was such a bad game," he said.

"We're in third place now."

"I can tell when a player's pressing. A talented player will show his talent even when he's having a bad game. You looked pretty good up at the plate, even though you didn't get any hits. I liked the way you stepped into the ball and didn't bail out when that left-hander crowded you."

"They've been crowding me since I got here," I said. "That ball has been crowded into my legs, my ribs, my ears. . . ."

"You don't like it here, do you?"

I shrugged. "You know how it is."

"We sent you here because this club needed help."

"This whole town needs help," I said.

"If you're really unhappy, we have a club in Wisconsin. . . ."

I looked at him, straight into those dark glasses.

"You'd send me there?" I asked.

"I spoke to Lloyd about it. He said he didn't think you were happy here. . . ."

I'd never told him that. Maybe I was unhappy, in some ways. But I'd sure never told it to Lloyd. So that was how he was going to unload me, get the trouble off the team, make life easier for himself.

"But he asked me not to send you to Wisconsin," Bonninger said.

"He did?"

"He said you were settling in now and doing the job. He felt it would do more harm than good if we juggled you around at this point."

"Lloyd said that?"

"So we're going to let you finish the season here. Is that all right with you?"

"It's all right with me," I said.

"You see, Johnny, we try to do the best we can for our players. We thought this league would be best for you, as far as breaking in was concerned. What local people think and do is beyond our control."

"I know that," I said. "And what I think and do is beyond their control."

He laughed. I made him laugh. The chief scout.

CHAPTER 11

In the next week or so, though, I thought maybe I'd made a mistake in not going to Wisconsin. Some of the fans in towns like Gilmore and Freddington continued to be pretty rough on me. I thought I'd get used to it, but I didn't. I had my troubles right in Proctor, too. At every home game I'd hear the catcalls. To make it even stranger and more hurtful, the better I did on the field the worse the insults became, from those few who continued to make the insults. If I hit a home run or made a good catch or did something real good and professional on the field they would stand up and yell and cheer in such a mocking way that it was more insult than cheer.

I didn't know what my teammates thought about all this. We never talked about it. It seemed to be something that embarrassed them. I know that the yelling bothered some of them, because I knew they liked me; I got the feeling that some of the others looked on it in a different way. I think they felt that because I didn't answer back, just took it all and kept my mouth shut, I was being feeble.

But I knew what feeble was. Mr. Wilson had told me more about Langdon, why Langdon had finally packed his bag and quit. It had come about not from taking abuse but from all of a sudden trying to fight it, Mr. Wilson said. Langdon finally got so filled up with the abuse and the insults and the hate that he started to yell back at some of the fans. And you know what they did? (That was Mr. Wilson asking the question.) They laughed at him. They stood up and cheered him and mocked him with applause. That finished him, because he had tried to fight them in their way instead of his own. Feeble was trying to be strong and showing that you weren't. As long as you didn't show that, then you were strong.

Well, maybe I had to take the bad-mouthin' from the people in the stands, but I sure as hell didn't have to take it from one of my own teammates. There was one guy on the team, a pitcher named Ken Malden from Indiana, who never had much to do with me. I noticed he talked a lot to some of the other guys, but never to me. Once I got a game-winning hit for him and later, in the clubhouse, he came over and patted me on the shoulder, so soft I could hardly feel it. He wasn't having such a good year; in fact most of the few games we were losing were being lost by him.

One night in Freddington he was pitching and it was the last of the ninth. We were leading 3–1. They had two on and two out. The batter cracked a hit to left center. I ran over and tried to backhand it but the ball stayed down and went under my glove. All the time I was running after it I knew two runs would score to tie and probably the batter would go all the way around with the winning run. When I picked up the ball in deep left center and turned and threw it in I saw the man was already steaming into third. He came in and scored standing up.

That was bad. It was my fault, my error. And to make it worse, it had happened in front of that lousy Freddington crowd that always bad-mouthed me. I could hear them yelling and jeering as I ran in. When I reached the clubhouse I was just about shaking with anger, most of it aimed right at myself.

I had run in at top speed, wanting to hide myself in the clubhouse as soon as I could. I guess I got in there quicker than Malden expected, because when I came in I heard him say out to nobody in particular:

"That goddamned nigger."

Well, I never stopped moving. From the moment that ball had been hit I'd been moving: running across for it, then chasing it down, then running in when I saw I'd blown the game, coming across the outfield grass and the infield, running past our bench and right into the dressing room where I stopped running but kept moving, walking fast right up to Malden and, with the glove still on my left hand, swinging at him with my right.

He was a pretty husky guy but I hit him solid and he tumbled back. He would have hit the floor if he hadn't been close to the wall and stuck out his hand and got balance. Then, before anybody could do anything, he was right back at me, snarling and snorting. He had his own mad—he'd lost the game on an error by a black man, he didn't like black people, and he'd just been slugged by one. So he had a lot going for him. We were two real angry guys.

There's no telling what would have happened. We wrestled around for a couple seconds, then Peterson, the third baseman, and Morrison, an outfielder, who were probably the strongest guys on the team, stepped in and got us apart. It was too bad in a way, because both me and Malden wanted to fight, we needed to fight. What was inside us both at the moment needed a good brawl to get loose.

Peterson had my arms pinned and he marched me to the other side of the clubhouse, while Morrison kept Malden against the wall.

"Sit down, Johnny," Peterson said, making me sit on the bench.

Lloyd wasn't in there yet. He'd stopped to yell at one of the umpires about something and was the last one in off the field. He was going to have his own mad, after the way we'd lost the game. In fact that was the maddest and unhappiest clubhouse you ever saw.

It got dead quiet when Lloyd came in. He threw down his first baseman's glove and walked across to his spot on the bench like a hungry lion. Nobody said anything. The maddest and unhappiest clubhouse of all time became the quietest. The bus ride back that night was like a trip to the cemetery. I didn't give a damn about Malden. He was never my friend anyway.

That was the first thing that happened soon after Bonninger had been there and I lost my chance to go to Wisconsin. The second thing came a few nights later, in a home game against Cashville. They were the last-place team and we were giving them a good drubbing. I came up in the sixth inning, and already I had two doubles in the game. We were up by something like 11–0 and it had become a pretty relaxed game.

The Cashville relief pitcher was throwing a good hard fast ball. We had racked him up for four runs the inning before and I guess he was chewing on his own teeth. I led off, hoping for another hit. These are the kind of games where you fatten up your average, when all the pitcher wants to do is get the ball over the plate and hope you hit it at somebody.

But he had something else in mind. I should have expected it. When you embarrass a pitcher you have to hang loose. I'd forgotten about that, so when that fast ball came straight for my head like the Bronx Express, I froze. Then I tried to drop, but the ball got there first.

I was wearing a plastic helmet and that saved me from serious injury, but still I felt the thud and it was like a bomb going off inside my head. The whole world suddenly closed in around me like a fist and as I sank to my knees I lost consciousness for a second. But then I got up and started to walk to first base. The inside of my head was swimming.

When I got to first Lloyd came up to me.

"How do you feel?" he asked.

I looked at him, trying to focus.

"Okay," I said.

"I'll put in a runner for you," he said.

"No," I said.

But he was already waving to the bench and somebody was getting up and coming over. Then Lloyd took me by the arm and led me back to the bench. A few people applauded; they do that when an injured player leaves the field, just to make him feel better. There weren't many who applauded, just a few.

I sat on the bench and watched the rest of the inning. I had the beginnings of a headache and was feeling a little dizzy. I had to squint to be able to really see things, to see them so I could think about them.

After the inning was over Lloyd gave me permission to go to the clubhouse. I showered and dressed, then lay down on the bench. The headache was there nice and steady now, like an old friend, not sharp or mean but just steady, like a pulse. Old Mr. Fitzhugh, who hung around the team as sort of a trainer and handyman, came in and asked me if I was all right.

"Mostly," I said.

"You took a good shot there," he said.

He was telling me something I didn't know?

"You want ice for it?" he asked.

"No."

He was about sixty, a little guy who wore the team cap and jacket. Sometimes he bandaged you or put iodine on a cut or massaged your arm. That's what he did.

"I can give you ice for it," he said. He hated to let an injury get away from him.

"Okay," I said, giving him a chance to do something so he could feel he was earning his cap and jacket.

He went out and came back about five minutes later.

"There ain't any ice," he said.

"Thanks anyway," I said. I was lying there with my forearm covering my eyes.

"How about a drink of water?" he asked.

"No thanks," I said.

"Aspirin?"

"I'll just lie here and let it wear off," I said.

Water, ice, and aspirin were about his limit, so he went anyway.

Later, after the game, some of us went to Latimer's for hamburgers and Cokes. The guys were feeling pretty good about the easy win and were cracking a lot of jokes, but I was out of it. I just sat there like a real dummy. My head wasn't feeling too good. I ate only half my hamburger. Sometimes the laughter around me sounded close and at other times it seemed far away.

We sat around until Latimer closed, then went out. Most of the guys went home, but a few of us, Peterson, Squalls, and myself, hung around. It was such a beautiful warm night, with the stars all out, that we decided to take a chance and stay out for a while. By taking a chance I mean that there was a curfew. We had to be in our houses two hours after the end of the game. If you broke curfew and got caught it meant a fine, usually five dollars. Lloyd ran bed checks now and then, and the town was so small that he generally found out if anybody was out after curfew. Proctor was such a quiet place late at night that I felt a fellow should have got a reward if he found something to do after hours, not a fine.

"You all right, John?" Peterson asked.

"Why?" I asked.

We were sitting on the park benches behind the movie house. There was a nice warm breeze in the trees. I'd called home that afternoon and my mother said it was ninety-six degrees in New York. Harlem is a pretty rough place to take when it is ninety-six degrees.

"You've got a strange look in your face," Peterson said.

"He always has that," Squalls said.

"My head hurts," I said.

"You took a good whack," Peterson said.

"I'll be all right."

But even as I said it I suddenly felt the world go soft around me and I passed out. Just like that. It was the first time in my life any such thing had ever happened to me. It was the most peculiar feeling: there one second, gone the next. I must've begun to tumble off the bench because I can remember hands grabbing me by the front of the shirt.

When I came to—I was only out for a minute or so —they had me stretched out on the bench. My head felt like that baseball was hitting it again—that original thump was steady against it.

"You fainted," Squalls said. He was standing over me with his short, muscular arms squared off on his hips. Peterson was looking at me very serious, holding his chin.

"I did not," I said. "I was mugged."

"I thought Negroes are supposed to have such hard heads," Squalls said.

"We do," I said. "That ball would've killed a white man."

"Stop joking around," Peterson said. "This could be serious."

"Man," I said, touching the sore spot with the tips of my fingers, "I can tell you that for me it is *mighty* serious."

"We'd better get you to a doctor."

"Why?"

"You might have a concussion."

"That's right," Squalls said. All of a sudden he was serious now.

"I don't need any doctor," I said, sitting up. Or at least I thought I was going to sit up, because the minute I tried to I felt my head start to swim sideways against one ear and I flopped down again.

So they helped me to my feet and got me to walking.

"Where are we going?" I asked.

"There's a doctor on the next street," Peterson said.

"It's kind of late, isn't it?" I said.

It was, but they had made their minds up. I knew enough never to argue with people who have made their minds up to do a good deed.

They chugged me along to the next street and we began walking under the trees. There was a streetlight burning in the middle of the block. This was going to be a lot of fun, them waking up a white doctor at one o'clock in the morning to treat a black center fielder with a headache. I guess I knew more about the world than they did, which was too bad. I'd settle for less knowing sometimes.

"There it is," Peterson said.

We'd come to a lawn with an iron post on it. Hanging from the post was a shingle that said CURTIS CULLANE, M.D. It was his office and his house at the same time. There was a light burning upstairs, in the house part. I could see it through the tall old tree that reached up beyond the roof.

They helped me along the walk, up to the door. We went up two brick steps and stood there.

"Let me go," I said. "I can stand all right."

Squalls let go but Peterson kept one hand on my arm. With his other hand he reached out and pushed in the bell. We heard chimes go off inside, a little singsong of chimes. I could just see Curtis Cullane, M.D., put down the book he was reading, take off his glasses, look at the clock and say, "Oh, hell."

"Nobody home," I said.

"He's home," Peterson said. "That's his car in the driveway."

We stood there and waited. You never feel so dumb as when you're standing and staring at a door waiting for it to open. Then we could hear somebody inside. Then he began to unlock the door and even as he was doing that I was thinking: *Is he just going to unlock it and open it without asking who it is?* In Harlem nobody would ever do that; in none of New York would any-body ever do that.

Then the door opened and there he was, Curtis Cullane, M.D. He looked about fifty, kind of slight, with gray hair. He was wearing a white shirt without a tie and corduroy pants and bedroom slippers. He looked at me first, then at Peterson and Squalls.

"Dr. Cullane?" Peterson said. The man nodded. "We have an injured fellow here. He needs some treatment, I think."

"Which one of you is injured?"

"Me," I said.

He looked at me, steady. He did not have an un-friendly face, he looked kind of neutral. He wet his lips with the tip of his tongue for a moment, then shifted his eyes to Peterson.

"I do not take colored patients," he said.

"Why not?" Peterson asked.

Curtis Cullane, M.D., smiled, a sad little wisp of a smile.

"Never mind," I said. "I'm feeling better. Let's go."

I started to turn to leave but I felt Peterson's hand tighten on my arm.

"We don't know how bad he might be hurt, Doctor," he said.

"He got a bad rap on the head tonight," Squalls said. "I think you ought to examine him. That much at least."

The doctor was looking at me again. I gave him eye for eye. I showed him that I didn't care if he examined me or not. I didn't need his nonsense. All I had was a headache. A good one. It was a big, soft, slow throb now.

The doctor's lips parted like he was about to say something, then came together again, pretty tight, then opened again.

"Come in," he said.

We went into the waiting room.

"Go right inside," he said to me. He told Peterson and Squalls to stay in the waiting room.

He followed me into the office—I could hear his slippers going *whish whish whish* behind me on the bare floor—and turned the light on. He shut the door. There was a desk in one corner and some glass cabinets along one wall and a couple of examination tables. The tables were soft leather and covered with a white sheet that was tucked around just like you tuck in a cot bed. He told me to sit on one of the tables. Then he closed the blinds over the two windows. He seemed nervous.

"You were hit on the head?" he said.

"By a baseball," I said.

"By a—are you a baseball player?"

"Yes."

"With the local team?"

"That's right."

"You must be Johnny Lee," he said. "I've heard your name. Some of my patients have been talking about you."

I didn't want to tell him how funny that sounded. Here his patients were talking to him about me (saying nice things, from the way he said it), and here was I now, having to be examined in his office only after he tightened up the blinds.

Then he came over to examine me. He looked into my eyes with a little flashlight, then tapped and poked here and there. He checked my heart beat and even took my blood pressure. He said he thought my reflexes were all right and that I didn't have a concussion.

When he was finished he began putting away his equipment.

"How old are you, Johnny?" he asked.

"Seventeen."

"I played baseball when I was seventeen. Not professionally, of course, though I think I might have been able to make it. I was a second baseman. They said I was pretty good. But I knew I was going to go on and study medicine. So I pushed baseball from my mind."

"I could never do that," I said. "Push baseball from my mind."

"That's because you probably have a real talent for it. A person should never give up on anything that he has a real talent for. If you believe in something you stick to it."

"That's right."

He didn't seem to be such a bad guy. I don't think he understood much of what he was talking about. But maybe he did, because he seemed a little bit far away and unhappy for a second. I thought he was going to tell me I could go, but he hung back from it for a minute.

"I'm sorry," he said. "For what I said at the door." Then he laughed and rubbed at the back of his neck. "You must think that's very funny. Me apologizing to you."

"I don't think it's funny at all," I said.

"No," he said, serious all of a sudden, "you're right. But I can tell you something. It's progress of a sort, though for me I wouldn't call it progress, since I never felt . . . like some of the others. Do you understand what I'm talking about?"

"I'm not stupid, Doctor," I said.

"Of course not. I'm sorry. You see, however, that's part of the problem. I mean my even asking you if you understood. Do you see? Hundreds of years of the same problem. That's what makes the progress so slow. That's what makes any progress at all remarkable."

"Why don't you take colored patients?" I asked.

"Because the people wouldn't like it. It's as simple as that. I would lose my practice. It would dry up. And I'm too old to go back to baseball." He smiled a little when he said that. "There are a lot of people who feel as I do, but they're afraid."

"I don't see how a *lot* of people can be afraid of anything," I said. He gave me a funny look, and I said, "But don't feel so bad, Doc. I know some people in New York who don't like it because I've got white friends. And I know some guys who'd rather croak than be treated by a white doctor."

"But pain isn't black or white—pain is pain."

That was very good. I hope he remembered it next time a black man came to his door.

He didn't charge me for the examination. I guess that was one way of making himself feel better. I felt sorry for him. Can you imagine that?

CHAPTER 12

Then there was the story in the local paper. They had a whole column on the sports page about me, with my picture and everything. The writer was a young guy who covered all the home games (and now some of the away games, too, because we were running for the pennant). I read the story over and over, till I'd got it by heart. The story said that I was the best-looking prospect Proctor had had in years, that I had the look of a future big leaguer. The guy wrote that I had "a smooth, devastating swing, a powerful arm and the running speed of an antelope."

The day the story came out we were playing at home. After the game there were some kids waiting outside. There must have been about a dozen of them, black and white. They wanted my autograph. I was so surprised I hardly knew what to do. I thought of all the times I'd waited outside the players' exit at Shea Stadium, hoping to get Willie or Aaron and guys like that. I remembered how I felt, all the excitement, watching them take *my* pencil and scorecard, looking at their faces while they signed, because I was standing right next to them, listening to them breathe. I couldn't believe now that these kids were feeling even a fraction of the same thing.

They stood around me in a little crowd while I signed their papers and scorecards.

"Think you'll make it, Johnny?" one asked.

"I dunno," I said, writing my name.

"How many years you think it'll take?"

"You think you could hit big league pitching right now?"

"What kind of bat you swing?"

"How many home runs you gonna hit this year?"

I didn't know how to answer all of those questions, really. I just kept my head down and signed away, gave them all a Johnny Lee, writing it with stubs of pencils and with ballpoint pens. One kid even had a Magic Marker and asked me to sign my name big across a piece of cardboard.

I got to admit that I felt important. If you've never had anybody ask you for your autograph, then you can't know what I mean.

I was really hopped up that night. When I got to Latimer's the guys kidded me a lot, calling me Big League Johnny and things like that. Squalls brought a piece of toilet paper out of the men's room and asked me to autograph it for him. Koronski asked me to autograph his cigarette. Some of them asked me when I was going to the Hall of Fame. Somebody else asked how much I had paid the kids to wait for me.

We all had a lot of laughs and it was great, except that I was still a Class D ballplayer making $450 a month and had to hang my clothes on a nail in the club-house and ride a bus for four hours to play a road game. I was still having trouble hitting a good slider and was still overthrowing my cut-off man on relays, and even though I was averaging one stolen base every two games and had scored from second on an infield out a couple of times, I still didn't know how to slide correctly. I was hitting .330, but the big leagues were still a dream.

But that night turned out to be the craziest night of the whole summer, the night I signed my first autograph. Because that was the night Squalls had the fire-crackers.

Latimer had just closed and most of the guys had cut out and gone home. I was standing on the sidewalk with Squalls and Savage. It was another of those nice warm nights that seem to fade on down from the mountains like so much velvet, and we just didn't feel like packing in. Especially me, since it was pretty lonely out at the Wilsons'. Everybody else had a roommate, and there was one house where six of the guys stayed. They used to sit up all night and play cards or talk or listen to records. But the landlords didn't let black people in there.

"What do you want to do?" I asked Squalls.

"I'm gonna buck the curfew tonight," he said. "That's what I'm gonna do."

I looked at Savage. He shrugged his shoulders. He was a big, slow-going guy who generally got his activities from Squalls' ideas.

"All right," I said. "I feel like bucking the curfew my-self. But what are we gonna do?"

"Wake up the town," Squalls said.

"What do you mean?" I asked.

I'll tell you what he meant. He had a pocketful of firecrackers. Some kid he knew in town had sold them to him. He showed them to us now. He had two cherry bombs and two packets of salutes.

"What are you gonna do with them?" Savage asked.

"What do you think?" Squalls asked.

"But where?" Savage asked. "You'll wake up the whole town."

"So what?"

Savage shrugged.

We walked over to the main drag, Jackson Street, and stood there. It was quiet as ever, not a sound, not a thing moving, not even the wind. You got the feeling the wind passed high over this town, so as not to shake any leaves. I still had never got used to such quiet. In Harlem you could always count on at least a transistor going or a car horn or somebody yelling, even at four o'clock in the morning. So to blow up firecrackers in this quiet seemed to be a real wild thing to do. There seemed to be something holy about the absence of noise, like the whole place was like the inside of a church, or a cemetery, or something.

The next thing I knew Squalls had struck a match and was holding it to the fuse of one of the salute packets. The fuse took fire and started to hiss. Squalls threw the firecrackers into the street and I watched the fuse burn there. I didn't think it would go off. I honestly didn't. I thought the quiet would be too powerful, wouldn't allow it, would smother it out.

But nothing seems sacred anymore, not even the quiet of midnight in a small town tucked off in the mountains. Because that quiet went bust like it never had before,

I'll bet. The firecrackers started to rip off one little blast after another. It sounded just like the movies of the Vietnam front lines you saw on television. It sounded louder than it probably was, too, because it was the only noise. I figured they were hearing it up in the mountains, too, all the hillbillies sitting up in bed and looking around their bedrooms.

We stayed there till it stopped. Then we ducked into one of the side streets, laughing so hard we could hardly move. We sat down in an alley and just laughed, punching each other on the arm.

"Let's put one under Lloyd's window," Squalls said.

"Smart," I said. "So he can get up and hustle a bed check."

"Let sleeping managers lie," Savage said.

We could see lights pass on Jackson Street. That was the cops, no doubt. I bet they'd speeded up that car now; this was the biggest thing that had happened in town all summer.

"Where next?" Squalls asked.

"I know where," I said.

We walked through the back streets, then over to Jackson again. It was empty. Dead quiet. The quiet had come right back and covered everything up again, just like the water covers up the hole you make in it when you throw in a stone.

I could see him sitting in there behind the desk. He was facing sideways. I knew that face well, and not just from the time he wouldn't give me a room. I'd seen him on the street a few times, walking like the ghost of Jefferson Davis or somebody.

"How are you gonna do it?" Savage asked.

"Just throw it in," I said.

"You'll wake up the whole hotel."

"So what?"

"That's right," Squalls said. "So what. That's what we're here for, isn't it, to wake up the whole hotel?"

Savage shrugged.

"Who's gonna throw it?" Squalls asked.

"You light it, I'll throw it," I said.

"That's right," Squalls said. "You've got the best arm on the club."

We were standing across the street from the George Proctor Hotel, with its neat lawn and shrubberies and spotlights rising up and shining on the big painted sign over the entrance. There wasn't a light on in any of the six floors. There would be soon, though.

Squalls handed me one of the cherry bombs. I held it up in the air while he lit the fuse. The second it took I fired it. It went on a line across the street and bounced once at the entrance and rolled into the lobby. I froze for a moment, looking at the mummy behind the desk. He was just leaning back, like he was tipping his chair over on two legs.

The explosion was louder than I thought it would be. It didn't go wide and far because it was inside; it went in a quick *Boom!* The guy behind the desk went over with his chair, from the shock I guess. Anyway, he was there one second and gone the next.

And then we were gone too. We went running for the closest side street. Lights went on in a few houses, popping little yellow squares here and there. We kept going until we reached the park behind the movie theater. We fell down on the grass and just rolled around and laughed.

I guess we were laughing so hard that we didn't see the lights until it was almost too late. Maybe they had heard us laughing—the quiet had come back, you know, and you could hear a laugh for a half mile. But anyway the lights came into the street, toward the park. Savage saw them first and jumped to his feet.

"Cops," he said.

It had to be cops. Especially when you know you've done something wrong. Then it is always cops.

We were up and running then. The park was pretty long, almost like a football field, with a clearing at the other end. There were trees on one side and that's where Squalls and Savage ran, though I didn't know that till the next day when I met them at the ballpark. I kept running straight ahead, fast as I could, my chest thrown out and my fists pumping a mile a minute.

I heard somebody yelling at me and once I threw a look back over my shoulder. I could see him running after me. The car was still parked where I'd last seen it, so they'd got out to come after us on foot.

I just kept running. So did he. Yelling all the time for me to stop. I went tearing out of the park and into the clearing. There was a streetlight up ahead and I didn't want to run through it where he could see me, so I cut off over to the left and ran into the street. From there I turned a corner and ran across Jackson Street, a couple blocks up from the hotel. There were lights on in it all right, on every floor. I crossed Jackson and ran into the next street, then doubled around behind the hotel. There were lights on in the back, too.

I kept running till I was gone out of breath. Then I went into somebody's alley and sat there in the dark and tried to fill up with air again. I just sat there and listened. Once the police car came down the street but they didn't see me. After about an hour I left the alley and started for home, real careful. I wondered what happened to Squalls and Savage. By the time I reached the Wilsons' I was sure I was going to find the cops waiting there for me. But the place was just as dark and quiet as ever.

I went in through my entrance and lay down on my bed. After a couple of minutes I started to laugh. No laughter tastes better than the laughter you have after you've gotten away with one.

But it wasn't over. When I checked in at the ballpark the next afternoon Lloyd called me into his office. He got behind his desk and sat down and looked up at me.

"We're deducting five dollars from your next pay-check," he said.

"Why?" I asked.

"For breaking curfew last night."

"Me?"

"You and two others, only I don't know who the others are."

"How do you know it was me?" I asked.

"Because," he said. "Because the cop that chased you was a young guy who just a few years ago was the fastest man they've ever had on their high school track team. When I heard he'd been outrun by a mile I knew there was only one person who could've done it. So I'm ninety-nine percent positive it was you. If I was one hundred percent, I'd fine you twenty-five dollars."

"I'll settle for the five," I said.

CHAPTER 13

It wasn't till the middle of August that I met Jenelle. She was related to the Wilsons—"kin" they liked to call their relatives—and I met her one night in Churchville, which was the black section of Proctor.

Churchville was off by itself on the edge of town and was what some of the locals called a slum. It was pretty run down, but was hardly a slum, at least not by what I'd seen in New York. Of course you can't judge anything by what you see in New York, since everything there is bigger and deeper and wider and taller, including the slums. Churchville was a couple of blocks of old wooden buildings and a few stores and three churches. You never saw any white people here except for the police, who drove by once in a while.

Old Mister Wilson had been pushing me to go over and see his kin. The kin was a cousin or something, but it wasn't until he started to talk about Jenelle that I started to listen. I guess I'd become kind of lonely, in spite of the friends I had on the club. I had a few girl friends in New York and we wrote letters back and forth, but that didn't help any.

So I went to see the kin one night. They lived upstairs from a store-front church. They were nice people, kind of formal, who treated me like I was the rich uncle from Kansas City. It seems they weren't at all interested in baseball, but they'd seen my name and picture in the papers and figured I was something special-made. Then I saw Jenelle. I was wiped out at first sight.

She was the daughter. She was sixteen. She was just beautiful. I could see myself walking down 125th Street with her. The kin might have been boondocks types with no education, but they saw right away that all bases had been touched and they went into the kitchen and left me sitting on the couch with Jenelle.

She didn't say much, but she always watched me when I was talking and there was a niceness in her eyes. I big-mouthed it, of course, telling her all about New York City and Washington, D.C. (where all I'd done was hang around the bus terminal). Then I told her about the big leagues, where I was going to be employed one day very soon, and jet travel from coast to coast, and being on television and in the magazines and things like that. I talked and talked, telling her about home runs and outfield assists and going from first to third on a short hit to left and beating out bunts and getting a jump on the pitcher and how to hook slide. All those things that girls like to hear about. I just sat there and talked on, steady as an open faucet.

"I've never seen a game," she said, when I had finally turned off for a minute and given her the chance.

"You've never seen a game?" I asked, my voice going high, just like she'd said something unbelievable.

I made her promise to come the next night. I hoped the autograph kids would be there again. (I hadn't signed any autographs since that first time. I guess in a town so small there are only so many who collect them and you get it out of the way all at once.)

Well, I was more nervous than when Bonninger, the chief scout, had been there. I tried not to think of Jenelle sitting in the grandstand with her kin (her father) and I didn't look at her once, because that wouldn't have been professional. I struck out twice and popped out twice, which wasn't very professional either. Especially after I'd been trying to hit four home runs. We won the game, Savage throwing a shutout.

But Jenelle thought I was wonderful. She thought it was so great that I had hit the ball so high.

"But it was a pop-up," I said.

The kin, the father, told me I had done just fine tracking down those fly balls. I'd made one good running catch in deep center, but Jenelle couldn't get over the fact that I'd been able to hit a ball straight up in the air, and so high.

"And with the bases loaded," I said.

"Yes," she said, as if that was wonderful too.

When we all left the park together after the game I found Squalls and Savage and a few of the others waiting for me.

"Can we have your autograph, Mr. Lee?" they asked.

I guess they'd found out that I had a girl at the game and so here they were, pumping me up. But they played it very cool and serious, handing me pens and bits of

paper and standing very solemn while I signed. Jenelle
didn't recognize them out of uniform and she was most
impressed. I couldn't tell if her father was on to it, but
if he was he didn't say anything.

"Thank you, Mr. Lee," they said after I'd signed.

"You're welcome, boys," I said.

"Good game," Squalls said, giving me an innocent
look.

"Thank you, son," I said.

The next morning Jenelle packed a lunch and we
went off to the mountains to spend the day. She had a
bicycle and I borrowed one from the Wilsons. It was a
nice, bright August day. We pedaled along the highway
until we came to a dirt road. Jenelle said she didn't know
where it went, so we took it.

We biked our way along until the road got to be
little more than a path. Then we got off the bikes and
walked them. The path became real narrow and was getting steeper. Finally we left the bikes hidden in the trees
and walked. She was carrying the lunch basket in her
other hand, the one I wasn't holding. I wasn't holding
her hand steady, just now and again, taking it like it was
by accident.

When we found a nice spread of grass we opened up
our blanket and sat down. I stretched out and stared up
at the sky, chewing on a piece of grass, while Jenelle got
the lunch ready. She had made some sandwiches and
brought a thermos of milk.

She wasn't much of a talker. That was a good change
after some of my New York girl friends. She was shy and
smiled a lot and sometimes would just drop her head

sideways toward her shoulder and look at you, then smile out again.

After lunch we took a walk and found some water. I called it a lake but Jenelle said it was a pond. We took off our shoes and socks, rolled up our pants (she was wearing jeans) and waded in. The water was cool. There were some flowers floating on the top. Jenelle said they were lily pads.

"How do you know?" I asked.

"I know," she said.

"You know about ponds and lily pads. I'll bet you know everything about these mountains. What's the name of that bird over there?"

She looked toward where I was pointing.

"What bird?" she asked.

I kissed her on the cheek. She looked quick back to me, like a scold, but only for a second. Then she smiled.

"You're the brave one," she said.

"Every time," I said.

We waded farther on, toward the middle of the pond. The water nowhere came higher than our knees. Then the rocks started to come. At first I thought it was a fish, some kind of jumping fish. But that was only for a moment, because then I realized they were rocks. About five of them hit the water around us, splashing up.

When I looked around I saw four guys standing on a rise of ground overlooking the pond. They looked like hillbillies; one of them was even wearing that farmboy outfit I'd seen on some of them—plaid shirt and over-alls. They were laughing. One of them threw another rock, which landed near and got water on me. I saw that was what they wanted to do—get us wet. They weren't trying to hit us. But that didn't make me feel any better.

"Knock it off," I yelled at them.

"Shhh," Jenelle said. She was scared.

I started coming out of the water. Another rock landed near me and got my pants wet. Now I was out of the water and stood there looking up at them. Jenelle was still in the water and they started throwing rocks around her. I picked up a few small stones. I fired one over their heads and they stopped. They looked back at me. They didn't say anything. Then they disappeared.

Jenelle was all upset when she came out of the water.

"Why'd you throw at them?" she asked.

"Why'd they throw at us?" I asked.

We put our shoes and socks on and went back to the blanket. Jenelle was just folding it up when they showed in the trees. I saw them moving real slow, the shadows on them. The one in front was the biggest. He was about eighteen, I figured, and was near to my height, which was just under six feet. When he got closer I saw he had a little toothbrush beard at the point of his chin.

"Hey," he said, "what's the idea of throwing at us?"

"You all were throwing at us," I said.

Now another one spoke out. He was the smallest, though he looked older than the big one. He was the farmer one. He had a few teeth missing in front (punched out, I'd bet) and yellow-looking eyes.

"Yeah," he said, "but there's four of us and one of you."

"There could be a hundred of you," I said.

"Pretty tough, huh?" the big one said.

They were all moving closer. The other two were

younger, with corn-colored hair that stood straight up.

"You made me wet," I said to the big one. "My girl, too."

"We didn't see you," the big one said. The little one laughed. Laughing, he sounded like some people do when they're sick. The other two just stared.

"I didn't see you either," I said.

"You're pretty smart," the big one said, pointing his finger at me.

We all just stood there looking at each other like a convention of wooden Indians. Then the little one said:

"Say, ain't you Johnny Lee?"

"That's right," I said.

The two younger ones blinked a couple times.

"You're Johnny Lee?" the older one said. "Why, I was out there the night you stole home."

"I was out there too," I said. "Only the umpire didn't catch it."

"Son of a gun!" the big one said.

Then we stood there an hour and talked baseball. They came to a lot of the games, they said. They were the Rost brothers, Dave, Leo, Dan, and Don. Each one was a real hot fan. They wanted to know if we could catch Gilmore and take first place. No Proctor team had ended up in first place in ten years.

"I was telling my old man," the big one said, "you're the best-lookin' darn ballplayer they've had here in years, I didn't care what."

I knew what he didn't care what about.

We all went back down the mountain together, still talking baseball. The big one even rolled Jenelle's bike for her till we got to the road. Then we said good-bye, after they made me promise to look for them at the next home game. Then Jenelle and me started to pedal back to town. It was all well and good, I was thinking, but suppose I hadn't been a baseball player?

"I'm so glad you were Johnny Lee," Jenelle said as we pedaled along.

"I've always been Johnny Lee," I said.

CHAPTER 14

The pennant chase got real hot as we came down to the end of the season. We'd actually gone into first place for one day but then dropped out again when we lost a doubleheader to Mariontown. Our home games were drawing an average of five hundred people and they were yelling their heads off for us.

I was still having my problems. The pitchers were still throwing at my head, but this time it was different. I'd got real hot in the middle of August and pushed my average up to .350 and was hitting off all the pitchers, lefties and righties.

"They're throwing at you because they're scared of you," Lloyd said.

There were brush backs and dusters and outright bean balls. They threw at my head and my body and my legs. My body was covered with bruises but I hung in there. I figured it would hurt more to be chicken and that anyway I had all winter to rest up, so I continued to stand with my toes right up against the plate and cock that bat and not give them anything. And then one night I got the real story from a black pitcher who was an ace with Cashville.

His name was Ack Norman. He was a stringy fellow from St. Louis who could pump fast balls for nine innings and not raise a sweat. Sometimes I'd talk to him before a game and we'd tell each other our miseries.

I homered off of him the first time up in one game late in the season and smiled to myself as I toured the bases, figuring I'd give him a good razz the next time we talked. When I came up for my second time at bat the first thing I knew he'd reared back and let go one of his buzzers straight for my head. I was so surprised I just barely bailed out in time.

I'll never forget that feeling of hitting the dirt. I was sore as hell. He'd done it on purpose and I couldn't believe it. After all, he was supposed to be my friend. I got up on one knee and looked out at him. He was standing there plain as a wooden Indian. I was going to yell to him: "What's the big idea, soul brother?"

But then I realized something. Sure he was my friend, and I was his—but all the same, hadn't I just ripped him for a homer and wasn't I trying for another? That's why he'd fired at me—and I guess that was why a lot of others were doing the same thing. The hot hitters always went into the dirt a lot. That's what Ack Norman was telling me with that fast ball.

I stood up and looked at the ground for a few seconds. I think I got my first real deep feeling of belonging then. It was a peculiar way for it to come, but it came in a way that would make remembering certain: fast and sudden and no doubts about it.

Everybody was worked up to fevers. I couldn't remember anything about what happened each day except the ballgame. What I did, where I went, with whom—it all was wiped out, all except the game. I didn't begin to come alive until I reached the park and suited up and ran out onto the field. Then I began to feel this terrific rushing inside of me, something that kept me high and anxious and eager and moving. There was nothing I couldn't hit, nothing I couldn't catch. Then, after the game, it took me a long time to wind down. I'd just sit in the clubhouse and stare into space, for the longest while.

One afternoon I went biking with Jenelle and I was so keyed up that I pedaled like a madman and left her miles behind, and had to wait a good half hour for her to catch up, after I'd remembered about her.

The season came down to Labor Day. That was it, the end. (The season ends earlier in the low minors than it does in the bigs.) We had a doubleheader with Gilmore at their park. We were one game behind and had to take two to win first place.

The bus ride out there was pretty quiet. The guys just sat with their thoughts, looking out of the windows at the mountains and the farms and the few houses we passed now and then. Behind us was a whole stream of cars and pick-up trucks. It seemed that half of Proctor was following us, coming to see these last games. Every so often I turned around and looked at them. It seemed they went a mile back, there was so many of them.

When we got to the park there were hundreds of people already there. Cars were parked all over the place. The lot was full and they were parking across the road in an open meadow. We got some boos and hisses as we stepped off the bus and headed for our clubhouse. But none of us took notice, nobody looked up; it wasn't professional to look at those who were bad-mouthin' you.

When we had suited up and were out on the field a couple of photographers came over and asked me to pose with Biljoe Mason, who was Gilmore's leading hitter, with a .355 average. They brought him over to me behind the cage. He was a southerner, from Georgia. He talked slow but moved fast and hit the hardest line drives you ever saw. One of the picture snappers asked us to pose shaking hands.

"I can't do that," Biljoe said in his cracker drawl.

"Me neither," I said. "I've got friends too."

Biljoe looked at me with a slow southern grin, not friendly and not unfriendly either. So we stood near each other while the photographers got their pictures.

You never heard such cheering, once the game got under way. They seemed to be yelling on every pitch. Our people were bunched up behind our bench and it was crazy to hear them yelling across at the Gilmore people. There were jokes and wisecracks and insults. I knew a lot of money was being bet, though I didn't want to think about that.

Well, the first game was a laugher. We took the pressure off in the third inning and ripped it wide open with seven runs. Peterson hit one out with two on, which was the big hit. That made it pretty quiet over on the Gilmore side. The only thing they could say was that there was another one to play. We took the first one by 11–2.

The second game was a different bag of cats. There

was nothing until the sixth inning, when they got a run. Then in the top of the seventh, with two out, Lloyd stepped in. He probably had more riding on this than anybody else. It would look good for him if the club won the pennant. The minor leagues are different from the bigs. Everybody likes to win, but it's more important in the minors for the individual to do well. Sometimes guys even root against their teammates, like an outfielder will root against an outfielder, or a right-handed pitcher against a right-handed pitcher, because there's only so many in each category that the big team can move up. But for Lloyd, winning was the important thing, because it looked good for him if he wanted to move up as a manager.

So, as the saying goes, he managed like crazy. He hit a home run and tied it up. He didn't hit many home runs, for a big guy, but he really laid into this one. He hit it over the fence in dead center. It was probably the longest ball I'd seen hit all season.

We went into the ninth tied at 1–1. I led off. Their pitcher was Harrison, the big string-bean left-hander. He was firing buzzers all game, had struck out ten so far. He always pitched me tight because I liked to crowd the plate. He came in too close and winged me on the leg. I knew it wasn't on purpose because the last thing he wanted to do was put a man on in that spot.

I hit the dirt and lay there like I'd been shot. Lloyd and a few others came running out, including old Fitzhugh. He had smelling salts in one hand and an ice pack in the other.

"You all right?" Lloyd asked me after they'd helped me to my feet.

"I'm okay," I said.

He walked with me down the line. I was limping.

"Do you want me to put in a runner?" he asked.

"I'm fine."

"You're limping."

"I want them to see it," I said.

He looked at me shrewd.

"All right," he said. "You're on your own."

I made a big fuss of flexing my leg at first base. I bent over and rubbed where I'd got hit—which you're not supposed to do—and the Gilmore big-mouths yelled at me and waved handkerchiefs.

Harrison went into his motion. Normally he watched me real careful because I stole a lot. But this time he had got it in his head that I was a wounded soldier and no threat to go. So he was just a shade casual. The second I saw him look at the plate, even before he committed himself, I was off. I burned up the line toward second. I watched the shortstop running to cover, his eyes glued on the peg. I watched his eyes and knew the peg was coming to the away side of the base and so I threw a hook slide, hitting the dirt and grabbing the bag with my left leg as I swung my body away from the tag. I was in on a close call.

When I stood up to brush myself off I could hear our people yelling up a storm. Harrison was standing on the mound with his hands on his hips, staring real mean at me.

The next man grounded out to the right side and I went to third. They walked Peterson on purpose, hoping to set up a double play on Lloyd, who was next. He was slow and a ground ball would probably do it.

I watched him as I led off third. He was really digging in and concentrating. I watched his face as he pumped the bat back and forth. His mouth was drawn tight. He was blinking his eyes a lot, too, as if he was trying to get them set, too. I knew how much this meant to him. Suddenly I felt my whole body getting excited with the idea of scoring. I wanted to bring it home for him. I hadn't thought much about it, but I knew that I liked him, that he had worked hard and helped me a lot, that he was a good baseball man who really didn't care if his players were black or white. There were some, like Clidell Hapgood and a few of the players, who just didn't like blacks, but I knew—now, all of a sudden, thinking about it at that moment—that Lloyd wasn't like that. He treated everybody equal. He was tough, he was fair, he didn't say much, and he wanted to win.

He hit the first pitch. Talk about not liking me. It almost tore my head off as it went whistling down the third base line like a rocket. I turned around as I trotted home and saw it landing fair, way down in the left field corner. Peterson went to third and Lloyd to second. Squalls blooped one into right center for two more and that was it. We won, 4–1.

The ride home was like a parade. With the bus in the lead, the cars and pick-up trucks were stretched out behind us, their horns blowing like crazy. It was about eleven o'clock at night when we all rolled into Proctor and the horns kept blasting away. I can tell you, that was one night the town wasn't quiet. A few cars rode up and down Jackson Street blowing their horns until the cops came and told them to shut up or else.

I had promised Jenelle I would see her when we got

back to Proctor, but I never had the chance. She had come to Gilmore with the Wilsons and her family and I told her I'd see her tomorrow, before I left.

The whole team stuck together. And it was great. All the guys seemed to want to be together. It was like we were a family, everybody was everybody else's brother.

We went to Latimer's. He had a table full of sandwiches and soda waiting for us, saying it was on the house. We were one hungry team and ate ourselves full. We kept the juke box going and sang songs. A lot of the local people came in and out to congratulate us and shake hands and things like that. Some of them came up to me and shook hands and told me it was a great season and wished me luck.

Lloyd left early. He pulled me to one side and shook my hand and told me I had had a great season. He told me, too, that I had a bright future and that he was sending a good report on me up to the front office. Then he told everybody he hoped to see them all next spring, and he left.

At about two o'clock in the morning somebody got a bright idea and we pooled some change and made a long-distance call to New York, to Scarsdale, where he lived. Bonninger, I mean. The chief scout. They got his number from information and I swear ten guys crowded into the phone booth. Peterson was elected to do the talking and I was pressed right in next to him. I could hear the phone ringing and all of a sudden it hit me that we were waking up the chief scout at two o'clock in the morning. Then I heard a voice say hello.

"Mr. Bonninger?" Peterson yelled, the way people do when they're talking long distance.

"Yes," Bonninger said. His voice was quiet. I could tell he hadn't exactly been awake.

"This is the Proctor ball club," Peterson yelled. "We're calling to tell you we just won the pennant." With that everybody cheered, so loud I couldn't hear what Bonninger said till Peterson asked him what he had said.

"I said, that's wonderful," Bonninger said.

"We just wanted to tell you," Peterson said.

"Yes, yes, I know," Bonninger said. "Congratulations to all of you."

"More money next year," somebody yelled from behind.

"Major leagues," another one said.

I whispered to Peterson, "Lloyd."

"Oh yes, Mr. Bonninger," Peterson said. "We want you to know that Lloyd did a great job all year. He helped us all a lot."

"He's a good man," Bonninger said.

We talked some more and then the money dropped and the operator came on to tell us the three minutes were up. We said good-bye, everybody yelling it in, then hung up.

"He said he'll see us all in spring training next year," Peterson said.

We got very quiet then. Because we knew it was over now. We'd gone out and played the games and we had won and we had celebrated and now it was over. We were just kids, rookies, but still we knew something about pro baseball. You never see the same unit of guys back together again the next year, especially in the minors. Guys get released, sent to other clubs. We were never all going to be together again.

Some of the guys were planning to leave first thing in the morning, driving or taking buses here and there around the country. To Florida and Texas and California and Colorado and Vermont and Michigan and Wisconsin. They'd leave their uniforms behind, their Proctor uniforms, and take only their spikes and gloves back, to be put away in the closet for the winter. Some of the guys had had baseballs signed by everybody as souvenirs. I got one, and it was very precious to me.

We all stood out on the sidewalk after Latimer had closed. Then some started to drift off, after saying good-bye and shaking hands and saying good luck and promising to write over the winter and saying they'd meet again in the spring.

Then I was standing alone with Squalls and Savage.

"We'll never forget this, huh, Johnny?" Squalls said. "I mean when we're in the bigs and winning the World Series and all, we'll never forget this, huh?"

"Never, man," I said.

"Did it all really happen?" Savage said. "That's what I want to know."

"It happened," I said. "Man, did it happen."

Then they walked off in one direction and me in the other. It was the last walk alone at night to the Wilsons' and it wasn't lonely. I wound up a few times and threw phantom baseballs, catching phantom runners. The patrol car came past, rolling slow and easy.

"Hey," the driver said, waving to me.

"Hey," I yelled, waving back.

I knew one thing: I wasn't going to sleep that night.

I was going to lie in bed and stare at the dark and listen to the quiet and watch it all happen again, just like the inside of my head was a motion picture screen.

Tomorrow morning Jenelle would be at the bus to say good-bye, and maybe some other people too. Then that long ride back to old Harlem and New York City. I was going to wish away the autumn and the winter and make it spring again, make it baseball time. I started wishing right then, on the quiet, nighttime streets of Proctor, in the Blue Ridge Mountains of Virginia. I was wishing so hard that all of a sudden I got the feeling that I could just reach out and touch the springtime.

DATE DUE

NOV 1 6 1993			

THE LIBRARY STORE   #47-0103 Pre-Gummed